Not Just Ano.....

THE MAILLY LE CAMP BOMBER RAID

by
Molly Burkett and Geoff Gilbert

Molly Burkett

Dedicated to those who failed to return and to
the French people.

ISBN N° 1 903172 51 9

Published © 2004 BARNY BOOKS
Text © Molly Burkett
Design © **TUCANN**_design&print_

Published by BARNY BOOKS
Hough on the Hill, Grantham, Lincs Tel: 01400 250246

Produced by **TUCANN**_design&print_
19 High Street, Heighington, Lincoln LN4 1RG - Tel & Fax: 01522 790009
www.tucann.co.uk   Email: sales@tucann.co.uk

INTRODUCTION

The Allied Commanders were already thinking about invading Europe as the last of the British army was being evacuated from Dunkirk. On June 22nd. 1943 the head planners at COSSAC (the Chief of Staff to the Supreme Allied Commander) were instructed that the main landing for the invasion, code named Overlord, was to take place on the Caen beaches during the hours of daylight. By the 2nd of July, the outline of the plan was evolved and the proposed target date was May 1st 1944.

COSSAC's plan for Overlord set out three conditions.
1. The overall reduction in the German fighter force
2. To limit the number of effective German offensive formations in France
3. To provide adequate sheltered waters.

The first two became the responsibility of the R.A.F. and U.S.A.F. The directive that became known as the Casablanca directive was code named Pointblank and was issued to the U.S. and British Bomber Commands. They were instructed to bomb airfields and aircraft assembly points, strategic rail centres, selected enemy coastal defence batteries, Crossbow targets (V weapon sites) and naval installations, particularly those within 130 miles of the city of Caen. But they did not want to rouse German suspicions about where the actual landings were to take place. They did not want them to move their Panzer Divisions into the Caen area. The designated landing beaches were top secret. There were only a few officers and top politicians who knew the exact position. Operation Taxable helped to confuse. This was a two to one policy. For every one bomb dropped in Normandy, two were to be dropped in the Pas de Calais area towards the Belgian border to make the enemy think that this was where the landings would be made. Many of the German officers were sure that the landings were going to take place near Calais. Hitler always thought the allies would land on the Normandy beaches and wanted to move troops into that area but he was overruled by his own Generals.

By the end of April, 1944, 30 attacks had been made on 27 targets in the Normandy area with 6,969 tons of bombs dropped on target. From May 2nd bombing raids were to be increased on specific targets. On the night of the 3rd-4th of May, bombers from 1 and 5 groups set off to attack Mailly le Camp.

MAILLY LE CAMP
Memories of a Bomber Raid

It was a bright moonlit night and, at 21.30 hours, May 3rd. 1944, the first Lancaster took off from East Kirkby airfield and set out for France to be followed by eleven more bombers from 57 Squadron coded DX. and 13 from 630 Squadron. They were also based at East Kirkby and coded LE. They flew steadily towards Mailly le Camp, which was where the 21st Panzer Division was stationed. This was a raid that the airmen had been told would be a piece of cake and which turned out to be one of the biggest bomber disasters of the Second World War.

The Lancasters from East Kirkby were joined by others:

From Bardney	No 9 Squadron - 15 aircraft
Dunhome Lodge	No 44 Sqdn - 13a/c
Fulbeck	No 49 Sqdn - 14a/c
Skellingthorpe	No 50 Sqdn - 15a/c
	No 61 Sqdn - 14a/c
Coningsby	No 83 Sqdn - 10a/c
	No 97 Sqdn - 9a/c
Metheringham	No 106 Sqdn - 9a/c
Spilsby	No 207 Sqdn - 17a/c
Waddington	No 63 Sqdn - 12a/c (RAAF)
	No 467 Sqdn - 10a/c (RAAF)

All these squadrons were from No5 Group and made up the first wave.

The second wave set off shortly afterwards and all aircraft were airborne by 22.25 hours. They were from No1 Group and were made up of squadrons from

Wickenby	No 12 Sqdn - 18a/c
Grimsby (Waltham)	No 100 Sqdn - 10a/c
Ludford Magna	No 101 Sqdn - 19a/c
Elsham Wolds	No 103 Sqdn - 14a/c
	No 576 Sqdn - 18a/c

Kirmington	No 166 Sqdn - 24a/c
Binbrook	No 460 Sqdn (RAAF) - 17a/c
North Killingholm	No 550 Sqdn - 18a/c
Kelstern	No 625 Sqdn - 15a/c

5 Special Duties Lancasters from No 192 Squadron at Binbrook

In addition, there were 2 Oboe equipped Mosquitoes from No 8 PFF (Pathfinder Force), 6 Mosquitoes and 3 ECM (Electronic Counter Measures) Halifaxes from 100 Group.

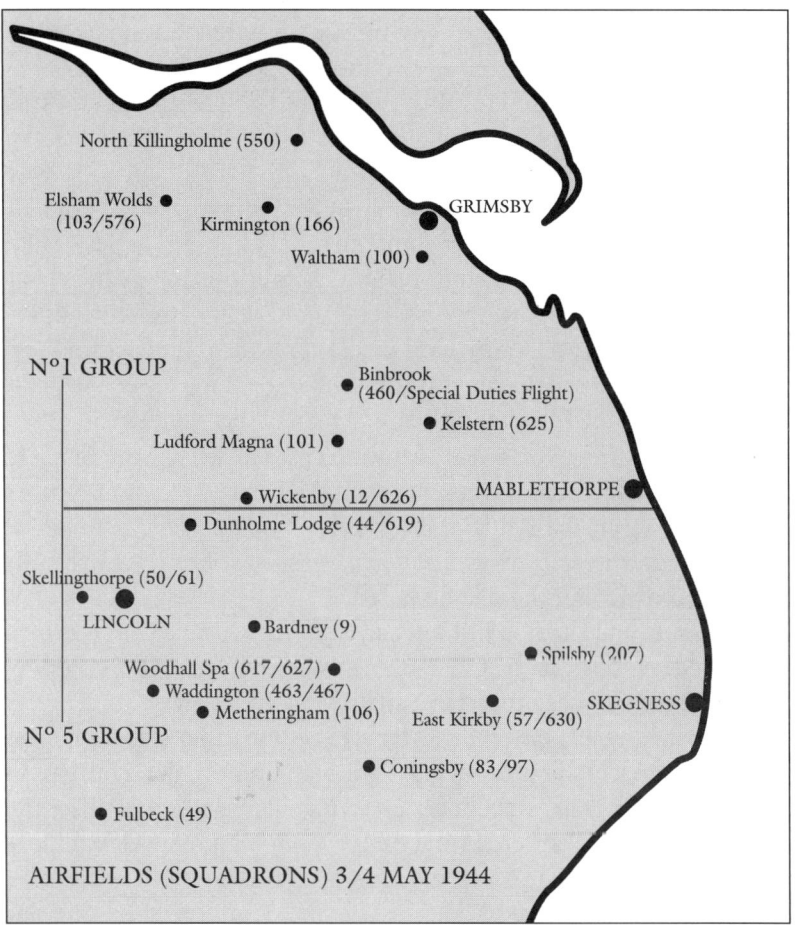

AIRFIELDS (SQUADRONS) 3/4 MAY 1944

Mailly the Camp is situated 128 kilometers south-east of Paris between Troyes and Challons. It would seem to be a small, peaceful village where little has happened over the years but on the night of May 3rd. it became the target of one of the most memorable air raids in the history of the area.

Mailly le Camp was and is a French army camp and covers an area of fifty square miles. It was in the 1890s that it was decided that the area surrounding the village of Mailly would be an ideal location for a military camp because of its position and suitable area for training although no major building work was started until 1902. There were many arguments before the first barrack block was built, arguments about where the buildings were going to be built and what the camp was going to be called but these were resolved and the first gun was fired at the camp in July of that year. The camp was used for military training so much so that the village itself became known as Mailly le Camp. The French were one of the leading countries in the development of powered flight in the first decade of the century and, in 1912, a squadron, known as Camp de Mailly Squadron was formed at the southern end of the camp under the command of Captain Bordage. Airplane hangars were built there. These were the very early days of military flying and some bizarre experiments were carried out such as dropping 'bombs' that were no more than petrol cans filled with water. The French army used the 75 mm cannons of which they were extremely proud. General Joffre visited the camp to see the guns in action as did the Minister of War and many other dignitaries.

During the First World War, many men passed through the camp. In 1914 it was under threat when the enemy advanced to within several kilometres during the Battle of the Marne. It was at Mailly that one of the new secret weapons was first seen, the special heavy tank. Mailly was the ideal site for them to be tested.

The army and airforce still worked together when the war was over but it became obvious that the site was not large enough for both of them and the airforce moved to a site several miles away.

After the French surrender in June 1940, the camp was taken over by the Wermacht and occupied by a battalion of the 21st Panzer Division as well as other tank units that had been sent there for regrouping. It was an ideal location for them with the well equipped workshops and large training grounds. Many men were trained there. The Germans considered Mailly a safe and comfortable posting and soldiers were often sent back from the African or Russian fronts to have a break from hostilities. Older people in the village still tell stories of the despair of some of the soldiers when they were ordered back to the front and how many of them would get hopelessly drunk on the night before they left. One of the tanks the Germans brought to the camp at Mailly was the new 503 tank, the Konigstiger.

Local people had become suspicious of the increased traffic in the camp and members of the French resistance had sent messages to London to tell the office there of their suspicions. Military Intelligence sent passes and papers that would allow the holder to be admitted into the camp and, in March, Raymond Basset had used a false police warrant which had been supplied by London and presented himself at the main entrance. The personal risk was enormous. He knew what would happen to him if he had been caught. Dreadful stories were told of how people had been treated by the Germans. Those that were caught spying were shown no mercy. Raymond Basset stands in my mind as one of the bravest men of this time and a true representative of all those French men and women who made up the French Resistance movement.

He drew charts and maps of the camp from memory and passed them on to an agent in Chalons-sur-Marne who then transmitted them to London. This was a target that fitted into the exercise code named Pointblank, the destruction of sites that offered specific threats to invading troops and could cause problems during D day by allowing German reinforcements to reach the beaches or sites that offered specific problems.

All operations were planned at Headquarters, Bomber Command at High Wycombe in Buckinghamshire, Specialist officers assembled every morning under the aegis of the Senior Air Staff Officer (SASO).They waited for the arrival of the Commander in Chief who, at this stage in the war was Sir Arthur Harris, generally known as Bomber Harris although he was known as Butch Harris by the airmen because of his "up and at them" approach, which reminded them of the bulldog called Butch in the Tom and Jerry cartoons that were popular at the time.

The senior Intelligence Officer would give initial assessment of results if there had been a raid the previous night but the main impetus was for the planned operation for that night. The senior Meteorological

Officer would outline the weather prospects and indicate which areas would offer the best chance of a successful raid. (Weather forecasting was not the sophisticated science that it is today).

A discussion would follow and a target selected. Details of petrol load and bomb load would be decided in conjunction with the maximum all up weight that particular bombers could lift. The general planning allowed heavy bombers to have a fuel reserve that would allow two hours extra flying to enable diversions to be made if their own base went out, generally owing to weather conditions. Lighter bombers would have reserves for one hour.

The decisions would then be transmitted to the various groups' headquarters by secure teleprinter transmissions. Most of the important passages would be encoded, especially the name of the target. Time on and off target would also be specified and the aircraft effort that was expected would also be encoded.

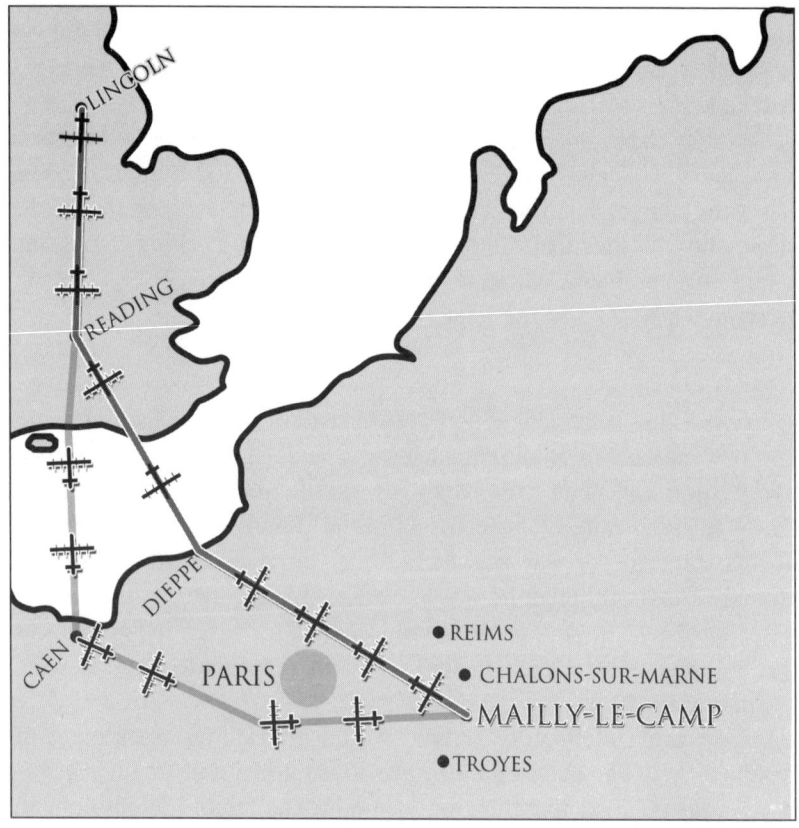

The groups would then have an Operations Planning Conference and group stations would be notified, This link would be provided on scrambled lines and only officers who had been cleared for security would be allowed to listen in to the discussion. The operational order would then emerge.. In the case of 5 Group, a time would be agreed for each turning point of the route and the individual navigators had the responsibility of sticking to these timings, normally by adjusting air speeds. Bombing tactics at the target would also be agreed and any other details that Group Staff officers or Station Commanders wished to raise.

Individual stations would then issue a Battle Order. This listed the individual crews operating that night, each crew member being listed on the Battle order. It would detail the briefing times for each category and the time of the general briefing when all detailed crew would assemble in the main briefing room. The messes would note the time of the pre-operational meal and the Station Catering Officer would put in hand the necessary preparations for the aircrew flying rations. These would be delivered to the crew room before the aircrew assembled to dress for the operation. The rations would be in individual cardboard boxes and marked for a particular aircraft and one of the crew would collect this along with two large thermos flasks, one containing tea and the other, coffee. The empty thermos flasks would be collected from the aircraft by the catering staff the next morning.

Crews could be called on to operate on two successive nights but it was unusual to be called for a third consecutive night although an individual crew member could be called upon if sickness had ruled out an aircrew member of his particular grade to make up a crew.

Occasionally, generally on winter nights, a raid would be cancelled, often when crews were ready to go out to their planes. It was at those times that they would realise how tensed up they were before a raid.

This was how the raid on Mailly le Camp on May 3rd, 1944 was developed.

• • • • • • •

No 5 group was the first wave of bombers and was to attack the south east part of the camp. No 1 group made up the second wave. Their target was the north west section of the camp. Thirty aircraft were to concentrate on an area near the workshops.

9

3. 101 SQUADRON.

SECRET.   MAILLY LE CAMP   BATTLE ORDER - SERIAL NO.505.   WEDNESDAY, 3RD MAY, 1944.

OFFICER I/C SQUADRON OPERATIONS: S/L. MORTON, D.F.C. & BAR.

	CAPTAIN.	F/ENGINEER.	NAVIGATOR.	W/OPERATOR.	AIR BOMBER.	M/U GUNNER.	R/GUNNER.	SPECIAL
K.	F/L.Todd.	Sgt.Powell.	F/L.Castle.	F/O.Wiggers.	P/O.Bardell.	Sgt.Whittle.	P/O.Ricketts.	P/O.Day.
D.	F/L.Knights.	Sgt.Parry.	Sgt.Innes.	P/S.Brealey.	P/S.Morgan.	Sgt.Armishaw.	P/S.Hart.	P/O.Cross
W.	F/O.Vaughman.	Sgt.Ormerod.	P/O.Corrin.	Sgt.Crandoll.	P/S.Westby.	Sgt.Dunsbury.	Sgt.Nunn.	Sgt.Manuar
C.	P/O.Forsyth.	Sgt.Holt.	F/S.Champayn.	P/O.Lund.	Sgt.Bates.	P/O.Dowdeswell.	P/O.Morn.	F/S.Eby.
B.	F/S.McHattie.	Sgt.Maxwell.	Sgt.Hall.	P/O.Allison.	P/O.Sutherland.	Sgt.Bloach.	Sgt.Exelby.	S/t.Forge
Z.	F/L.Kaura.	Sgt.Webster.	P/O.Shannon.	S/t.Crawford.	Sgt.Spoart.	Sgt.Claremoor.	Sgt.Wareford.	O.Phase
FIVE	F/O.Muir.	Sgt.Rogers.	F/O.Bell.	Sgt.Horrigan.	P/S.Duir.	Sgt.Lords.	Sgt.Hogh.	Sgt.Sher
X2.	F/O.Davidson.	Sgt.McClure.	Sgt.Jacobs.	Sgt.Woods.	Sgt.Bishop.	Sgt.Barton.	P/O.Garm.	
H.	F/O.Maloby.	Sgt.Fuxor.	Sgt.Hurst.	Sgt.Hurst.	Sgt.Barchau.	Sgt.Hayman.	Sgt.Johnson.	P/S.Lawri
B.	F/O.Fillingtham.	Sgt.Goodliffe.	F/O.Loquariah.	Sgt.Mosley.	F/O.Connell.	Sgt.Saulsby.	Sgt.Lo.	P/S.Mark
T.	F/S.Davidson.	Sgt.Broomhead.	F/S.Barnfather.	Sgt.Hall.	Sgt.Anderson.	Sgt.Day.	W/O.Degg.	S/t.Gloury
F.	P/O.Arnold.	Sgt.Webb.	F/S.Rowbottan.	Sgt.Orr.	F/S.Greenaway.	Sgt.Watson.	P/O.Winfield.	P/S.Bombe
K.	F/S.Flintoft.	P/S.McDonald.	F/S.Bradbury.	Sgt.Fulton.	Sgt.Carey.	Sgt.Mokorology.	Sgt.Grouthan.	Sgt.Harri
I.	F/O.Baker.	Sgt.Cro.	W/O.McNaught.	F/S.Whitchord.	F/S.Hacklett.	Sgt.Ridgway.	P/O.Blair	
I.	F/O.Rippon.	Sgt.Smith.	Sgt.Skinard.	Sgt.Whitchord.	F/O.Lynham.	Sgt.Stack.	Sgt.Hunter.	F/O.King.
L.	F/O.King.	Sgt.Parrott.	P/O.Henger.	F/O.Worts.	F/O.Moore.	Sgt.Bathgate.	F/S.Williams.	Sgt.Child
V.	F/O.Osborn.	Sgt.Sugar.	F/S.Butler.	Sgt.Strava.	F/O.Noble.	Sgt.Williams.	P/O.Brown.	Sgt.Doyle
C.	P/O.Cirriam.	Sgt.Dak.	P/O.Kilian.	Sgt.Johnson.	W/O.O'Regan.	Sgt.Chambers.	Sgt.Horac	
A.	W/O.Drow.	Sgt.Rodway.	F/O.Brenner.	Sgt.Dudley.	Sgt.O'Connor.	Sgt.Haymon.	Sgt.Divine.	P/S.Walke
G.	RESERVE AIRCRAFT.				Sgt.Morrisan.	Sgt.Walter.		

WINDOIS: F/L.BULLOCK AND CREW.

ALL CREWS NOT ON BATTLE ORDER ARE TO REMAIN IN CAMP UNTIL AFTER TAKE OFF.
TIME OF ORIGIN: 12.15 HOURS.

(Sgd) C.B. Morton, Squadron Lr
Commanding, No. 101 Squ

Wing Commander Leonard Cheshire was the marker leader with three other Mosquitoes from 617 squadron. They were the experts in marking confined and difficult targets. In the winter of 1943 – 4, Cheshire had been given the task of training crews to perfect low level marking techniques. He was at his shrewdest when he selected experienced members of bomber crews for the task. Air Vice Marshal D.C.T. Bennett was violently opposed to this new concept of target marking and these views were shared by many of the officers who served under him in 8 Group (PFF – Path finder Force) after the return of 83 and 97 Squadrons to 5 Group. The two Pathfinder squadrons that had returned to 5 Group in April 1944 did not like the idea of marking being undertaken by the Mosquitoes. They saw themselves being reduced to "flare carrying" forces. This was an attitude that was carried by a number of air crew a long time after the raid had been committed to history.

Marking started at 23.58 hours. Zero hour was 00.05. The first two Mosquitoes arrived early at the rendezvous and flew on for thirty miles before returning to the site. Flares had already been dropped by 87 and 93 P.F.F. Squadrons and these lit up the area so that Cheshire, dropping to 1,500 feet from 3,000 feet, had no problem in locating his two red spot flares on target. Wing Commander Cheshire was a perfectionist and he wasn't happy with their position and called up Dave Shannon in the accompanying Mosquito to mark the site that needed to be bombed more accurately, dropping his red spot fires accurately at 00.06 hours. Cheshire told the Master Bomber to hold the main attack off until he was satisfied. After Dave Shannon had dived down to 600 feet to lay the markers, Cheshire gave the master bomber the go ahead.

According to the post operational report by Wing Commander Deane, the green target indicator dropped by the OBOE controlled Mosquito was timed at 23.59 hours and fell some 800 meters north of the centre of the target. Dave Shannon's marking was completed seven minutes later. The target was marked on time. It was then that communication difficulties arose and things began to go badly wrong.

The Master Bomber tried to pass on the order but his words were distorted. In some cases the radio frequency was jammed by an American broadcast. Only a few of the Lancasters picked up the garbled message and went in and bombed, and so did a handful of other planes with experienced pilots who realised that delaying

11

dropping their bombs and circling the yellow datum point that had been laid near the village of Germinon could be dangerous..

Wing Commander Deane knew that the delay in starting bombing by the main force was serious. He tried to send the message by morse but it failed to transmit. It was found out later that his radio was 30kcs off frequency although it was never proved that this was one of the causes in the breakdown of communications.

Squadron Leader Sparks was the deputy master bomber and he had been instructed to only take over if the master bomber was shot down or he was given instructions to do so. He obeyed those orders.

Cheshire realised things were going badly wrong and tried to get a message through to bomb. He then tried to abort the raid but failed.

Meanwhile the Luftwaffe controllers had called up their fighter stations. Two well known fighter bases at Chalons sur Marne and St Dizier were within 45 Kilometers of the target. Night fighters from these bases and also from Leon and Jurincourt became airborne. The 60 Lancasters waiting and circling above Chalons over the yellow datum point proved easy targets in the bright moonlight. Lancasters were already exploding in the air and crashing. Crews began to break radio silence demanding to know what was going on. Squadron Leader Sparks then gave the order to go in and bomb. It was like a stampede in the January sales. The order was five minutes late but that was an eternity to the waiting crews. They were anxious to drop their bombs and make for home but the German fighters were amongst them and they wreaked havoc.

1,500 tons of bombs were dropped in twenty minutes. By this time, 9 Lancasters were crashing in flames. Many of the German soldiers on the ground had sheltered in the woods when the first bombs had dropped and had returned to the camp, thinking the raid was over. They were not ready for the ferocity of the second wave and many were caught out in the open. Some dived into the trenches but that didn't save them. Many of them were buried as the sides of the trenches fell in on them or walls collapsed over them. Then the water tower was hit and the flood of water poured into the trenches, drowning some of the men who were trapped there.

258 airmen lost their lives on the Mailly le Camp raid and 42 aircraft failed to return. In addition 27 Lancasters were damaged, 24 by enemy action and three by being caught in the blast when bombers near them had exploded. Another Lancaster managed to return to

Elsham Wolds but was so badly damaged that it couldn't be repaired. Two days later Plt. Off. L Mouzon a Belgian Spitfire pilot brought back photographic proof that the camp had been almost obliterated. 114 barrack blocks had been either demolished or badly damaged. 47 transport sheds had been hit. 65 vehicles and 37 tanks had been destroyed. 218 German soldiers had been killed and 156 seriously injured. Reports from French resistance tells of the breakdown of morale amongst the Germans and of soldiers wandering round in a daze.

•••••••

We four Mosquito marker crews of 617 Squadron were surprised to be summoned to the briefing room at R.A.F. Woodhall Spa in Lincolnshire. during the afternoon of 3rd. May 1944. The whole aircrew strength of the Squadron had been briefed for Operation Taxable (the D Day spoof where we attacked and bombed mainly in the Pas de Calais area to make the Germans think that that was where the invasion was likely to take place). We were banned from all other operations until Taxable had been completed. It was at the briefing that we first heard of Mailly le Camp.

Mailly le Camp was a French tank training camp some 150 kilometres ESE of Paris. The camp was then occupied by the Germans, and French Resistance had sent a message saying that a German Panzer Division was temporarily bivouaced there en route to a position behind the Atlantic Wall. Allied Command was anxious that this target was hit before it could move out again.

This was to be a new form of marking. 617 were marking the targets and 627 were setting up the back up markers.

627 Squadron was the Mosquito squadron that had taken up target marking for 5 group. They had recently been transferred from No 8 (P.F.F.) Group and Bomber Command Headquarters felt that this particular target needed the expertise that 617 pathfinder marker crews had regularly demonstrated in finding targets that were difficult to locate by purely radar aids.

Since our Lancasters were not involved in the operation, it wasn't considered necessary to give these 617 marker crews the usual full Main Force briefing.. We were just given the elements that applied to the actual target area.- time of first flare fall, - timing of the first wave

The twin engined Mosquito could easily be mistaken for an enemy aircraft at night

of aircraft (this was to be 5 Group), - lull time for the marking of the area allocated to the second wave of aircraft, (No. 1 Group).

Wing Commander Leonard Cheshire was to be Marker Leader. The main emphasis for the Mossie crews was security. We all knew that the invasion could not be far away and security was tight. Intelligence seemed strangely disturbed about the four crews operating on this mission. In effect, the bottom line was, MARK YOUR TARGET AND THEN GET THE HELL BACK TO THE U.K.

Operation aircrew were encouraged to keep themselves up to date with all that was going on relating to the intelligence side of the R.A.F. It was all too easy to confine yourself to your own station and your own crew but it was important to know how you fitted in to the bigger scene. Without exception, the Intelligence section of an operational R.A.F station was comfortably furnished with very pleasant W.A.A.F. personnel and, if you were lucky, you would be brought a mug of tea as well. An intriguing amount of literature was always available.

I was browsing through some of the papers before the Mailly raid and I had come across an item which I had read and not thought about again, not until after the Mailly le Camp raid. A German prisoner of war had been interrogated and said that an operation order rested in the safes of all Luftwaffe day fighter squadrons in France code named WILDE SAU. This order was to be invoked when moonlight conditions were such that day fighters could readily be scrambled to operate in a freelance role during the passage of a bomber stream *over France. I noted the report and didn't give it another thought.*

The briefing took place in the afternoon and this was followed by an operational meal in the Petwood Mess (now the Petwood Hotel). We didn't talk about the operation. We had been briefed and we knew what we had to do. In any case some airmen were superstitious and considered it unlucky.

Wing Commander Cheshire and Squadron Leader Dave Shannon were detailed as markers for 5 Group. As C.O. and Flight Commander respectively, these two had their own transport. They took off some time before the Mosquitoes of Flt Lt Terry Kearns and Flt Lt Gerry Fawke. I was Gerry Fawke's navigator and my log book shows that we were airborne from Woodhall Spa at 22.30 hours.

As a navigator, my job was to keep the plane en route and inform the pilot of our position. The wind could affect the plane's flight and had to be constantly monitored. Wind is always the problem. A head wind could slow us down while a tail wind would speed us to our target. It could blow us to the left or the right of our planned course. It could speed us up or slow the aircraft down. or blow it to the left or right of the planned track. To compensate for the effects of the wind and still arrive over the target at the correct time, the aircraft may need to alter its speed or be pointed at a slight angle away from the intended track. The angle between the aircraft heading and planned track is known as drift. The speed and strength of the wind could vary at different heights and I would be constantly checking the course we were flying.

At the pre flight briefing, the met man would give us the force of prevailing winds and details of the weather we could expect. Once we were airborne, it was my job to calculate our exact position accurately.

We had been ferried down to the airfield in a 15cwt van driven by a W.A.A.F.. Parachutes and harnesses were collected from the locker room before we went out to the aircraft. The pilots had carried out their pre flight inspections of the exterior of the aircraft and the controls and signed Form 700 which certified that the aircraft had passed all the ground crew inspection and was fit to fly. The ground crew was as important part of the operation as the men that flew the plane and a close relationship had built up between us. The success of the operation was as much their responsibility as ours and they would be waiting, often anxiously, for our return. We settled ourselves in the Mossie and the order was given, "Chocks away." We taxied round to the take off point and took off.

The trip across England was uneventful. The Gee (*'Gee' used radio pulses from 3 ground stations to provide a navigational 'fix') radar aid was working well and the wind velocities were checked and logged. It was a lovely moonlit night without a sign of cloud at any altitude. We flew at 6,000 feet, a height reckoned to be reasonably safe from light flak and below the minimum height for the heavier stuff and it also enabled us to work without having the oxygen mask clamped over our faces. We crossed the English coast on time at Beachy Head and sped towards the French coast crossing just to the east of Dieppe.

It was while we were crossing the Channel that I realised how bright the moonlight was. The inevitable enemy jamming of the Gee radar had begun to invade the main time base but, at that stage, it could be read through without too much difficulty. I discovered that the moon was so bright I could map read accurately by its light. I could never recall doing such a thing before except perhaps when I had crossed the Alps en route for Italy in mid October 1942.

I used Gee very sparingly, mainly when there were no defineable pin-points.

An advantage of being in the second wave was that we could see the party starting well ahead of us and the final run in could be made by visually steering towards the action. The raid seemed to be progressing favourably. We had picked up no messages on the VHF frequency, neither did we have any invasion of the VHF by any outside broadcasting unit. Everything seemed as normal as one would expect on a raid of this size. Yellow route markers had been placed north of the camp at Germinon and I was really shocked to see them. These were to mark the datum point and they were visible from a long way off. Lancasters were already circling in the area waiting to be called in to bomb. If we could see them from that distance, so could the Germans.

Gerry positioned the Mossie for the targeting dive and we watched as sticks of bombs positioned themselves round the well placed markers. They had been placed accurately. I kept Gerry informed as the minutes ticked away. At the beginning of lull time, our Mossie was in the correct position, perfectly poised to make the marking dive. We had just commenced the dive without being actually committed to it when a stick of bombs exploded on the target. Gerry wheeled out of the

16

Sqld Gerry Fawkes, pilot and Sqld Tom Bennett Navigator beneath a Mosquito of 617 Sq.

dive and climbed to regain the altitude we had lost and to reposition the plane for the dive. Further bombs fell while we were doing this. We commenced our second dive and yet again sticks of bombs fell. I was not only shocked but appalled. In 617 squadron discipline was strict and we had grown accustomed to the rules. Timings were strictly observed. I took a very dim view of the lack of discipline that the main force were showing. I didn't appreciate the chaotic conditions that were developing above us.

As we sought to re-position, Gerry buttoned the VHF, "PLEASE STOP BOMBING. We are trying to mark for the second wave."

For the first and only time we heard another voice across the ether. "Well get a move on, mate," came a calm but firm Australian voice, "it's getting a bit hot up here," and this was the first indication we had that everything was not going according to plan.

No further fall of bombs interrupted the marking process and both Mossie crews laid their markers close to the new aiming point. We were to learn later that Terry Kearns and his navigator, Hone Barclay, had had a similar disconcerting marking experience. Our own 'friendly' bombs could have delivered us to German interrogations.

Satisfied with a job well done, we readily obeyed our order to cut and run and we set course for the return route. We had seen no aircraft shot down until we were on the first leg away from the target. Then

17

we saw the first ghastly sight of a Lancaster hitting the ground and exploding in flames. The fireball illuminated the pall of oily smoke that was always part of such a macabre scene. To our mounting horror and concern, that was not the only casualty. Again and yet again, the tragedy was repeated. I tried to convince myself that it was German night fighters that were being shot down but the funeral pyres were too large for that. When a fifth bomber was cremated beneath us Gerry said, "Not a healthy area for a twin engined aircraft, Ben, let's find another way home."

It was pandemonium in the air. Lancasters were jinxing in the sky trying to escape from the Meserschmitts and Junkers. Our gunners were aiming at the enemy but they could only hold the fighters in their sights for a few seconds before they had flown on. We didn't waste time. We were as likely to be shot down by one of our planes. The mosquito is a two engined aeroplane and could have been mistaken for a German night fighter in those circumstances. I gave Gerry a rough course for the nearest safe part of the coast and then busied myself in the niceties of tidying up to ensure that we crossed the coast at a reasonably safe spot. I could not exorcise from my mind the glimpse of hell we had seen or the thought of the crews that had been flying the planes that had crashed. Gerry and I didn't communicate with each other. We were too involved with our own thoughts. Then the words "WILDE SAU," came into my mind. Had the Germans invoked this? Certainly the weather conditions were everything that had been required. I pushed the idea to the back of my mind. There was an aircraft to get back to Woodhall Spa.

We landed at 02.30 hours on the 4th of May, 1944, silent and appalled at the carnage we had seen, all the more unbelievable for being associated with a French target. To everyone's relief, all four of the Mosquitoes returned safely. Most of the air crew had waited up to see us return, they were so concerned for our safety. The news was flashed through to Headquarters, Bomber Command as soon as the fourth plane landed.

It was in the debriefing room that we heard how disastrous the operation had been. That was when we first heard talk of interference on the VHF channel and a developing communications difficulty. We heard of Cheshire's despair as he tried to sort out the situation and how he had attempted to have the operation aborted. The two earlier Mosquitoes had not seen the carnage that we had witnessed. Dave Shannon's navigator, Len Sumpter, said that as soon as they were satisfied they had nothing more to contribute to the proceedings, they had headed for home. Pat Kelly said they had seen a couple of Lancasters shot down but nothing like the carnage we had witnessed. He was mollified by our eye witness description of the effectiveness of the first wave bombing but more concerned about the communications mayhem.

At our personal debriefing, I said to the intelligence officer, "I feel we have seen the activation of the German operation order, WILDE SAU."

He looked at me absolutely perplexed.

"Add it as a footnote, Arthur," I said. "I'm sure somebody at group or Command will fathom it," but there was never any reference made to it later.

Our worst fears were confirmed later that day – 42 Lancaster missing, 14 from 5 Group, the first wave, and 28 from 1 group, the second wave. My first reaction was that 5 group had stirred the hornet's nest and 1 Group had taken the stings. There was the one possible consolation. The target had been dealt a devastating blow and probably many lives had been saved on D day and beyond by the sacrifices at Mailly le Camp that fearful May night.

Squadron Leader Tom Bennett D.F.M
49 and 617 Squadrons 1942-1945.

• • • • • • •

19

OBOE

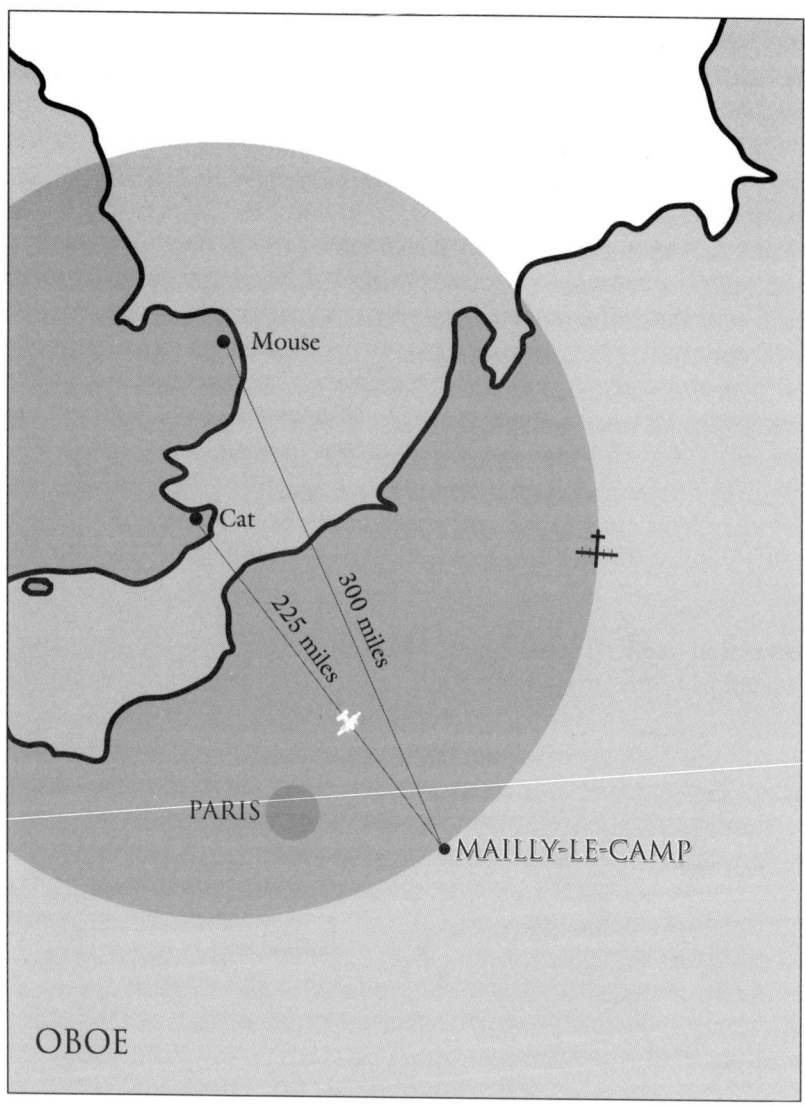

OBOE

The Oboe navigation system positioned an aircraft very accurately over its target, even when the target was hidden by 10/10ths cloud or at night.

It was operated from two radar tracking stations in the UK - the 'Cat' and 'Mouse' stations.

On a map, with Cat as centre, an arc of a circle was drawn, passing through the target (radius of circle in illustration = 225 miles). Radio signals from Cat ensured that the aircraft flew along this path. (If he was on course, the pilot would hear a continuous tone. To the right of the line he heard a series of 'dots' - if to the left he heard 'dashes').

The distance from Mouse to the target was also measured on a map - (300 miles in the illustration). All the time that the aircraft was flying along the path determined by Cat, Mouse was monitoring its own distance from the aircraft. When this equalled the target distance, the pilot was told that he was over the target.

In practice, two ground operators were required to handle one aircraft at a time and it was not practical to deal with a fleet of bombers in this way. So the use of Oboe was normally restricted to the pathfinder aircraft - usually Mosquitos. An advantage of this was that the range of Oboe transmissions was restricted by the curvature of the earth, but using the high flying Mosquito increased the working range to some 300 miles.

· · · · · · ·

We were posted to Elsham Wolds and work was quickly found for us, unloading bombs at the local railway sidings. We wore rolled up cap comforters on our heads, sweaters, overalls and rubber boots. It wasn't long before we graduated to packing four pound incendiaries into their canisters. We fitted fins to bombs of anything up to 2,000lbs and took the loaded trolleys out to the aircraft. We even worked in the fused bomb bays to which bombs were returned if a raid was cancelled. They were kept in special bunkers protected by high earth and concrete embankments. We thought nothing of riding out on the trolleys, straddling the fused bombs without a care. When we had a dull moment, we would try and liven things up by igniting some of the 4lb. Incendiary bombs. The larger 12lb incendiaries were fitted with a safety pin which had to be unscrewed to arm them. We found it easier and quicker to knock them out with an iron bar which was usually used to close the canister in which they were stowed. These drop bars became an essential part of our equipment. We all had one stuck in the long pocket of our overalls. It wasn't long before we were all allocated to other duties.

We became very sensitive to the changing moods of the station which swung from being easy and light hearted when operations were off, often when the weather was bad and many aircrew would pause and look at the gathering clouds gathering north of the Humber, to a palpable tension when the operation was on and the target was known.

When ops were scrubbed, a wave of relaxation spread across the station and buses or trains were provided to take crews into Scunthorpe or Brigg. Scunthorpe was a grimy steel town, lying in the shadow of vast slag heaps. There were three pubs, the Bluebell, the Oswald and the Crosby. It was generally accepted that aircrew N.C.O.s used the Bluebell. It wouldn't have been out of place in a Western. It had a large, open saloon bar with a sawdust covered floor and a raised wooden platform in the corner on which a man in a bowler hat played non stop. It only needed busty, silk stockinged girls to complete the illusion but the ladies provided did their best and this made up in humour what it lacked in propriety.

Peter Beechey - Air Crew Cadet

We thought nothing of straddling the bombs waiting to be loaded

Anyone who took part in the raid of Mailly le Camp on the night of May 3rd. 1944., will remember it as the worst operation of his tour. I certainly do.

The first problem was that there was a full moon and that meant that our primary protection –darkness – was missing. The second was that it had been decided in April that raids over France would only count as a third of an operation towards the thirty we had to make to complete a full tour.

We were told at the briefing that the target would be marked by 617 squadron and not by P.F.F. (Pathfinders Force) as was normally the case. This was because visual identification was necessary due to the compactness of the target and the close proximity of the village and French civilian population.

I was in 101 Squadron and we were in the second wave of bombers. We were required to circle a yellow ground marker dropped by pathfinders of 627 Squadron and await instructions from the master bomber to come in and bomb. As we approached the target, I could see Lancasters already orbiting the yellow ground marker. They showed up clearly under the full moon and they were being shot down at an alarming rate. The degree of brightness from the markers coupled with the light of the moon was enough for me to read their identification letters.

I suggested to the pilot that we held off from entering the orbit zone. It would have been suicide. Ken Fillingham, the pilot, called for Stan Liquorish, the navigator, to come up to the cockpit to advise. Stan was 32 and the uncle of the crew. Ken and I were only 19.

Stan came up and saw the massacre and his first words were, "My God, heads will roll for this. Dogleg north, 3 minutes."

It was an instruction the pilot didn't need repeating. As we turned north, I had already counted thirteen Lancasters going down, most of them exploding in the air as their bombs would have been fused since they were in the target area.

We dog-legged north for three minutes, then turned back towards the target. I am sure it was a manoeuvre that saved our lives. The German fighters had returned to their bases to be refuelled and rearmed but, by that time, they had already shot down a lot of Lancasters. We ran through the target and bombed, dropping 4,000 pounders which the second wave of aircraft carried. As the cookie left the bomb bay, the Lancaster lifted a good twenty feet now that it was relieved of that weight. The Luftwaffe gave us a rough ride before we turned for home. Of the 42 bombers that were lost that night, four were from our squadron.

Unfortunately the delay by the Master Bomber in calling in the

Left to Right standing: Ken Connell - Bomb Aimer, Phil Medway - W/Op, Ken Fillingham - Pilot, Dennis Goodliffe - F/E, Jack Soulsby - Mid Upper, Stan Liquorish - Navigator Front: Adrian Marks - Spec Op (ABC), Jimmy Law - Rear Gunner

second wave to bomb gave the German fighters a free shooting gallery and they took full advantage of it. This lead a number of pilots who were being attacked while orbiting the marker to break the golden rule of Bomber Operations to maintain radio silence. Messages were being sent to allow the Lancs to come in and bomb like, "Pull your finger out Master Bomber, we're dying out here," and one Canadian voice, "If this is a third of an op, I'm half way to LFM (Lack of Moral Fibre)." The delay was said to be caused by a breakdown in comunication between the master bomber and his deputy. It was claimed that an American Forces broadcast jammed the transmitters although we did not hear it but we did hear an Australian call out for those shouting abuse to, "shut up and give my gunners a chance." He was obviously under fighter attack and could not hear his gunners evasive action instructions because of those that were breaking R.T. silence.

We generally relaxed on our way back to base but not that day. The memory of the burning bombers was too close for comfort.

Denys Goodliffe - 101 Squadron Ludford.

As usual on the day of the raid, we went to the flight office after breakfast to see if the squadron was operating that night. It was and later on in the morning we were told that our crew was on the battle order. About 6 o'clock we had a flying meal of egg and chips and then a briefing when we were told what the target was and our take off time. That night it was Mailly-le-Camp. I had never heard of it but we all gave a sigh of relief as French targets were supposed to be easy. They only counted as a third of an op (operation). A normal tour (the number of raids we had to go on) was 30 ops. After briefing I went to the crew room and put on my flying gear. I wore long johns and vest, battle dress, kapok flying suit, gaberdine outer, heated gauntlets, socks, electrically heated socks (like slippers) and sheepskin boots. On top of this I put on a parachute harness and a Mae West or life jacket. I collected a parachute from the store and the crew bus took me and the rest of my crew out to the aircraft. We all climbed on. I turned left towards the tail and slid down the ramp to the rear turret. I settled in, plugging in my suit and the intercom that connected the headset in my leather helmet. The pilot called each of us in turn to check everyone was OK.

'OK Rear Gunner?'

'OK'. When he got a signal from the ground he taxied the aircraft to join the queue to take off. The time was 22.00 hours. There was a caravan at the end of the runway and, as each plane took off and cleared the runway, a signaller would flash a green Aldiss lamp to the pilot of the next plane.

We were one of the 19 aircraft that took off from Ludford Magna that night. The pilot followed the course he had been given at the briefing. We flew at 7,000 feet, the navigator checking the course and giving the pilot course corrections. On most raids I didn't hear any sounds over the RT (radio-telephone) but that night, as we got nearer the target, we could hear the Pathfinders talking to each other. We were ordered to circle some yellow flares on the ground north of the target. There were fighters active but I could only see dark shapes in the sky. I saw some aircraft explode and others go down.

Because I could hear the radios, I could hear the crews. I heard one man screaming, calling out for his mother and crying, 'We're going to die, we're going to die'. A voice answered, 'Be quiet, turn off your RT. If you're going to die, die like a man'. Everything went quiet. We were still circling round and round. It felt as though we were circling

25

for hours but it was probably only minutes. Over the radio I heard a voice I recognised from another aircraft asking, 'Hello Pathfinder, can we come in and bomb now?'

A voice replied, 'No, continue circling'.

It may have only been a few minutes but it felt like hours had passed when I heard the same voice ask the same question and get the same reply, 'No, do not bomb, continue circling.'

The voice, which belonged to Kit Carson who had a distinctive Canadian accent replied '.... the RAF, we're coming in'.

I heard one of the Pathfinders say, 'I've been hit. I've got to go down,' in such a matter of fact way as if he was saying he was going out for a walk. (I think he later escaped from France with the help of the Resistance).

At 12.32, after circling for what seemed like hours, we were called in to bomb. Our pilot Tom steered the aircraft straight and level over the target and the bomb aimer released the bombs as close to the target as he could. We turned back for home. We arrived back at our base at Ludford Magna last of our squadron and 12 minutes after the previous aircraft. We had already been chalked up as lost but the aircraft we were flying that night was slow. We disconnected ourselves and clambered out of the aircraft. The crew bus took us back to debriefing where we told an intelligence officer what we had seen and heard. The I.O. would have heard some of the radio exchanges during the raid from what he could pick up on the radio at the base. After debriefing, I went to the Sergeants Mess and had a meal, egg and chips again, and went to bed.

We found out later that the camp and 37 German tanks were destroyed but 42 out of the 350 aircraft which took part in the raid were lost. Soon after this raid, there was another, which also had heavy losses and after that, all raids on France were counted as one op.

Gordon Wallace

· · · · · · ·

Elsham Wolds lay high above the flat fenlands of Lincolnshire bounded by the Humber Estuary and the Weir Dyke to the north and it was cold. Out of the dark sky to the east came the wind. It was always there filling the windsock in the signal square and lifting the pennant on the runway

A debriefing

control van. It chilled the airmen gathered in groups on the perimeter track and ruffled the hair of the W.A.A.F.s who huddled in the shelter of the control tower. It also helped the Lancasters of 103 and 576 Squadrons take off, disappearing towards the dark sea, heavy with their fuel and bomb loads.

Those of us off duty would watch them taxi out. Most had their top hatches open and helmeted figures would be waving at those of us on the ground. Lancaster PM-L was known for the lavatory paper which streamed from the open hatches and the cloth caps pulled down over the helmets of the crew. W.O. Lewis's crew was Australian and, to them, the lavatory paper and the cloth caps was as much an essential to their safe return as the efficiency of the crew and the aircraft.

If we were off duty, we would go and get some sleep. Those who had slept would often get up in time to see the planes return. Everyone counted. Ground crews cheered and departed for their dispersal points as they recognised their aircraft. Congestion built up in the circuit but soon most would be down.

We were aircrew cadets and arrived at Elsham Wolds in March 1944. We were accepted by those on the station. They were experienced and used to the constant movement of airforce personnel.

I was attached to flying control and, after a few days in the control tower, I was given duty watch in the runway caravan. This was a big heavy, four wheeled caravan with a glass dome through which we could observe the runway. It was painted in black and white squares and was remote from the driver's cab. We were equipped with radio, binoculars, flares and Aldis lamps and we had a galley which housed a primus stove so we could keep ourselves well supplied with cups of tea.

The runway caravan had final authority over aircraft taking off and landing. We were in charge of the runway. We were the last to see the aeroplanes as they lifted into the air and, if we noticed anything amiss, we would notify the control tower. We would watch the aeroplanes lifting off and, when the runway was clear, signal with the Aldis lamp for the next one to follow it. The operation was so quick that Lancasters would leave at thirty second intervals as they did on the night of May 3rd. We waited for their return.

The telephone that connected us to the control tower rang to tell us the Lancasters were returning and some of them needed assistance. That sounded ominous.

We scrambled into the glass house. The fire engines and ambulances were lined up and then we heard the throb of the engines as the planes approached. Every thing else was forgotten in the excitement of landing over thirty Lancaster bombers, many of them badly shot up, some on three engines and demanding priority. That we got them to the ground with no further casualties was mostly due to the discipline and skill of the pilots but, to this day, I can remember the shock we felt at the state of some of them. The state of one stays in my mind to this day. Those in the tower saw her first and recognised the throes of a dying aircraft, tail down with the two propellers on the port side standing immobile. There was a gaping hole where the H2S should have been and there was something heavy and bulky hanging behind the tail wheel. There was no finesse in getting down. She came straight in, down wind, fast and low over the hedge and, as she hit the runway, the rear turret parted from what was left of the tail structure and bounced in a rolling arc towards those watching on the perimeter track. Crash tenders and ambulances were already racing across the grass towards the plane, veering towards it as its undercarriage collapsed and its wings and propellers gouged the ground. The Lancaster twisted, slid and stopped. The radio operator had been mortally wounded in the fighter attack that had crippled the aircraft. The mid upper gunner had jumped down from his turret to care for his wounded colleague and had dropped straight through the hole where the H2S had been. His chest type parachute was still in its stowage.

Pilot Officer Peter Beechey.

• • • • • • •

I was a balloon operator working at the docks at Jarrow. We were twelve girls on the site and it was hard work. A barrage balloon was 64 feet long you know and we had to learn everything about it and know how to manage it. They used barrage balloons to keep enemy aircraft away from important sites. We had to drive the winch and maintain the engine and we had to move heavy blocks of concrete. You needed those on a windy night to steady the balloon. We had to know how to splice a rope or wire and how to manage the gas, The barrage balloons were filled with gas. We had to keep the bowsers and do night duty as well.

Then I was moved to East Kirkby in Lincolnshire and that was where I met Arthur. He was a mid upper gunner and I worked in the sergeants' mess. It was a completely different atmosphere from the docks at Jarrow. There was a purpose and togetherness but over all, there was this terrific sense of humour and Arthur was the worst of them. He didn't take anything seriously. He would make light of everything although he knew I was worried when he was out on a raid. I would always go and wave him off. You could see the gunners up in

their turrets. I couldn't go to sleep. I couldn't rest until he was safely back on the ground.

You would know when there was going to be a raid because the guard would be doubled at the entrance and the gate would be chained. The men would report for their briefing and we would know from the looks on their faces as they left what they were going to face that night. Some of the men would hide their feelings with what I called the airforce humour. Others would look tense. You would think those that were nearing the end of their tour would be less worried but often these were the tensest of the lot.

I would count them coming in but mostly I would be out on the field watching and waiting. One day a Junkers 88 was in the circuit as they came in to land. It had followed them back from France and, as one of the Lancasters started its final run in, the German fighter shot it down – seven men dead. An order went out for the other planes to scatter but it was too late for that one.

One day, the crews were out at their Lancs ready for off when they were stood down for an hour, We were told to take refreshments out to them so my friend and I volunteered. She went out to 57 Squadron and I went out to 630. That was Arthur's. They were standing round waiting, joking while I poured out the tea. They were calling out to each other saying things like, "The Germans have got it in for you tonight but don't worry. We'll eat your egg and bacon for you."

There was always a fried meal waiting for them when they returned from ops. I couldn't stand it. It wasn't funny. I refused to go out to waiting air crews again. It upset me that much.

Nobody was worried about the raid on Mailly le Camp. It was just run of the mill but it turned out to be the worst one most of them had ever experienced. Arthur refused to talk about it. None of them made jokes about Mailly le Camp.

We were married for seven years. Arthur was taken ill and died. He was 32. The specialist thought that his war experiences had contributed to his death but, of course, they couldn't prove it.

If you go to The Aviation Heritage Centre at East Kirkby, go into the hangar there and look at the model of the airfield. My grandson made that and it has got Arthur's name on it and mine. I'm so proud of both of them.

Lilly Taylor. W.A.A.F..

• • • • • • •

I lived in Crofton near Wakefield and, when I left Grammar School in 1942 at the age of 16, I went to work on the railway, the L.N.E.R. I wanted to be a pilot but, when I joined the R.A.F. in March 1943, I was told that they weren't recruiting pilots, so I became a Flight Engineer and was posted to 166 Squadron at Kirmington in Lincolnshire in February, 1944 and joined the crew of Lancaster ME 749. I always

*Jacks
conversion unit
Lindholm 1943*

Jack aged 18

Le Oasis
The place where Jack sheltered a few nights and days. He was brought food here by the 'resistance'. We returned to this place in September 1971 and had another photograph taken.

said I had the most important job in the crew because I had to monitor and correct the engines of the plane. I needed to watch the dials and check the speed, pressure and fuel all the time and report to the pilot. We had four fuel tanks on the Lancasters and I had to make sure that the plane balanced as we used the fuel. I generally emptied the wing fuel tanks before I used those on the fuselage.

I flew on ten operations, eight of them to Germany. We expected the next one on 3rd – 4th of May, 1944 to be a piece of cake, Mailly le Camp, there and back in three hours, I never thought for three hours substitute four months.

It was a lovely moonlit night. We could see the countryside beneath us. We dropped the bombs and were beginning our return flight when, suddenly, the German fighters were amongst us. We took avoiding action but it was too late. We were hit and the plane caught fire and we were going down. The order came to bail out but we were already moving towards the exit. The order of bailing out from the bomb aimer's hatch was laid down, bomb aimer, flight engineer (me), navigator, wireless operator and pilot. The rear and mid upper gunner bailed out from the rear door.

My parachute had a faulty harness and was only attached by one main strap instead of two. That made the parachute lose air. It wasn't fully extended and I descended far too *fast. Luckily we had bailed out over woodland called Foret d'Othe. I landed in a tall tree and stayed there until daybreak. My first attempt to climb down resulted in me tumbling thirty feet. A lower branch caught my trousers and tore them but it held me firm. I jumped down to the ground and all that was wrong with me was a torn trouser leg and a bruised back.*

While I had been waiting for daybreak, I had seen a Lancaster crash into a field just beyond the wood. I had a good view of it from my vantage point. The first thing I did when I reached the ground was to make my way towards the crash site, thinking I might be able to get some identification mark from the plane but there were too many villagers around it so I thought it would be best to keep away and went back into the wood. That was where I met the woodcutter who asked me where my parachute was. He wanted to get it down so that the Germans would not know an airman had landed in the area and come looking for me but it was far too high and we had to leave it there.   We went to his shed in another part of the wood and he told me to wait there until he came and fetched me. It was after dark when he returned.

He took me to a house in his village and the next night, Polo, a member of the Maquis came for me in a car. I was driven to a farmhouse near another village and I stayed there for the night. The following day, May 6th., I was driven to another house and I stayed there for three nights..

I now know that I was being sheltered by M. and Mme Chevalier at Tharets in the parish of Cerisiers. All I knew then was that I was being cared for by two very brave people who would have been taken out and shot if the Germans had found me in their home. During the whole of my time in France, I was aware that I was continually being helped by many courageous people to whom I owed my life. It was nearly thirty years later that I met up with them and was able to thank them in person for their tremendous bravery.   I found it hard to come to terms with the fact that these people were putting their lives at risk for me. The war threw up many heroes but these French people were the top of the list as far as I was concerned.

A few days later, I was taken to a Maquis camp near Dixmont. I hadn't been there long when a motor bike drove up with a pillion passenger who looked familiar.. We stood and stared at each other. I found myself face to face with my own Aussie pilot, Garth Harrison.

33

We stood and stared at each other and then we were grinning and shaking each other by the hand. Neither of us had expected to meet another airman let alone one from our own crew.

A few days later, on May 15th, we were preparing to move camp. Two men had gone into the village to try and find transport but they had been gone a long time and the leader, Captain Castagne, was beginning to feel concerned. Andre Dussault and I were pulling down a tent in the forest. The others were loading the guns and equipment into a car. They were further into the forest, a short distance from the camp site. Andre and I were up in a tree unfastening a tarpaulin which was attached to the lower branches of several trees when we heard a warning shout from Frassetto who was the lookout at the crossroads. I shouted a warning to the others and clambered down but we were at a disadvantage. We had to get down to the ground before we could take cover and we didn't have the time. The Germans began to fire their machine guns. Andre was shot. He ran for several yards before he fell to the ground. The Germans continued to fire. As I hit the ground, there was another burst of gunfire and I was shot three times. Two of the bullets, one to my forehead and one to my chin, caused surface wounds. The serious damage was done by the bullet which penetrated the left side of my skull. I fell to the ground and lost consciousness. I was taken prisoner but I can't remember anything about what happened over the next few days.. The Germans took my two identity discs before taking me to the hospital in Sens.

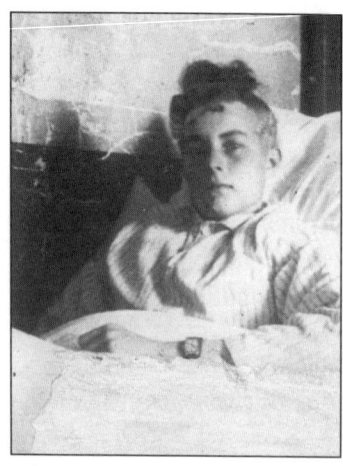

Jack in Sens Hospital
June 1944 aged 19

I can't remember anything after being shot until I came round in hospital ten days later. I didn't know where I was but I did know that I couldn't speak and I was paralysed down my right side. One of the doctors who operated on me came and showed me the X rays and that helped me to understand the extent of my injuries

There was one other patient in the small ward with me, Georges Mauclerc, a farmer. He looked after me. I found out later that he had got a message to the Maquis to tell them where I was. He was suffering from a self inflicted wound. That wasn't unusual then. Many French men were being sent to work camps in Germany and some would harm themselves, even amputating fingers, so that they couldn't go.

The staff in the hospital were wonderful to me. The surgeons were Dr Piquet and Dr Bonnecaze and Sister Mizaelle was the Sister of Mercy in charge. These three falsified my records of progress so that I could stay in the hospital because they believed that the Germans were planning to transport me to a prison camp where they knew I would find the conditions life threatening. A German doctor came to examine me on the 14th of June who, despite my very serious injuries, decided I was fit enough to be moved. It was imperative that I should be taken from the hospital before that could happen The French doctors told me to act as if I was daft and I thought I'd given a good performance but it obviously wasn't good enough to fool the German.

The Sister of Mercy contacted the Resistance. Gilbert Praz, their leader, quickly organised a plan for my escape. The Sister hated the Germans. She called them Boche. Her fiance had been killed in the First World War and she never forgave them. Until then I had only walked a few steps round the ward and, although I could make a few noises, I was unable to speak and tried to communicate with signs.

I had been told that the Germans would be coming to collect me the next afternoon and a guard was put outside my door to make sure that I didn't leave the room. This was very unlikely. I was still very weak and suffering from partial paralyis of my right side. I was also told that my French comrades would be picking me up in a van. During the late morning of June 15th, six men of the Resistance came for me. Four of them stayed outside the hospital to keep watch while the other two made their way to my ward. The guard outside the door was a policeman who was sympathetic to my escape. He handed his gun to the two men. One of my rescuers seized a blanket and put it round my shoulders and we made our way to the hospital entrance. I hadn't realised I was so weak but I needed the support of both men. Bernard gave the policeman's gun to the porter and told him to return it in ten minutes while Gaston helped me into the coat they had brought to hide my pyjamas and put a beret on my head. I felt weak and found walking difficult I discovered that they hadn't brought a van. They'd brought bicycles. I didn't have the strength to pedal properly. Two of the men, Gaston Charruet and Bernard Monamy, made a tremendous effort. One pushed me and the other pulled. I did what I could to help. I used my good leg to push the pedals round. I felt very vulnerable, a six foot man wearing clothes that didn't fit him properly being pushed along by men who barely reached my shoulders. At one stage, I noticed that the man pushing me was losing the gun from his belt. I made gestures to attract his attention and point it out. I still couldn't speak. There was a lot of German activity because the D day landings had taken place and it was necessary for them to keep the main roads clear to ease the movement of their SS Divisions towards the battle area. We were passing German troops all the way and the town was busy. We expected to be stopped at any minute. It turned out that it was a good job that they hadn't been able to get the van. There was a road block stopping all vehicles and searching them. I began to panic. I knew that if they stopped us it wouldn't only be curtains for me, it would be for those two as well. I needn't have worried. We cycled right through the road block None of the German soldiers spared us a glance. The safe house of Father Camus at Malay le Grand was some distance away and it took us twenty five minutes to get there. We had to go the long way round to avoid the Germans. I could hardly stand when I got off the bike. In the evening, two nurses came out from the hospital to give me the injections I needed.

The S.S. took up quarters in the district that evening. It was lucky that they didn't take over Fr. Camus' farm.

Bernard and Gaston started getting ready to move me early the next morning. My means of transport was a horse and cart filled with a mixture of manure and straw and a plough fastened behind it. It wasn't a comfortable trip and it was certainly a smelly one. In my weak state, everything seemed to go like clockwork. It did that day. A rendez-vous had been arranged with Raymond Chillinger. He drove the cart to meet a car which took me to the farm of M. Thorallier. The nurses and doctors came out regularly from Sens every night to give me the medication I needed so urgently. My condition was still causing concern.

I was taken from one safe house to another. Praz organised the movements and he seemed to have many contacts. They were wonderful to me. There was M Henri Pannequin known as Prudent, Serge Caselli (Constant), Amedee Caselli (Constantin), Mme Moreau, M. Delapierre, M. and Mme Douin and her two children who were similar in age to myself. Mlle Douin was so worried about my health

M et Mlle Merlette (Maman at Papa) are next to Jack. Mimi is next to the American soldier on the left her friend (name unknown) is next to the other GI. The blacksmiths forge at Chaumot on ;Liberation Day

that they called Doctor Bothereau of Villefrance Saint Rual to their farm to examine me, putting their own lives at risk yet again. Dr Bothereau was so concerned that he asked Dr Fort, a surgeon from Joigny Hospital to examine me.

I had to move away quickly from the farm. German troops had arrived in the area and were searching the neighbouring villages. Shortly after leaving the Douin's farm, the Germans arrived to search it. They found nothing but took a calf with them when they left.

The Bayard group, as they were known, led by Henri Pannequin, moved me to Saint Romain le Preux. I had only been there a short time when I was taken by a rival group to the Chateau de Saint Phalle at Cudet. They looked after me that night but I didn't feel as comfortable with them as I did with the group that I knew and trusted. The next morning, the Caselli brothers came to get me back and took me to M. Morrison's at Quatre Vents. It seemed that there was even competition between different Resistance groups. Sheltering allied airmen was extremely dangerous but it was also regarded as being prestigious. especially now that the allies were advancing. Moving from one place to another was always nerve-racking. There was always the possibility that we would be stopped by the enemy and the German soldiers were pretty nervous themselves now that their army was retreating.

We didn't only have to look out for the Germans, we had to keep an eye on our own side. Aeroplanes were always present in the skies and railways and important sites were being bombed. During one bombardment, I was in a cart covered with straw being taken to another safe house when a raid took place. The oil depot and the railway station were bombed. Everyone ran for cover but I couldn't.

37

I had to stay where I was. I couldn't help thinking that it hadn't been that long ago that I had been one of those men helping to drop the bombs.

Although my condition wasn't getting worse, it wasn't improving very quickly either. This was a cause for concern and, at one point, the resistance workers discussed shooting me because I was becoming such a liability. Luckily I didn't know anything about that at the time. I didn't learn about that until nearly thirty years later when I met up with my friends again.

We always felt at risk. On one occasion, Serge Roland and I were in the bake-house making meal for the pigs when two German soldiers arrived to requisition provisions. Serge dealt with them without giving a clue that I was hiding in the next room. Needless to say, when they went, he and I looked at each other and gave a sigh of relief. We didn't need to say anything.

I finally arrived at the home of M. and Mme Merlette in Chaumont in early August where I stayed for almost three weeks. They treated me like a son. M. Merlette was the local blacksmith. I had a tiny room with an iron bedstead which was so small that my feet stuck through the bars. I had to stay in bed on the days that Mme Merlette washed my clothes because they didn't have any spare ones to fit me. There was a door in the room that lead to the outside. This would have been my escape route if the house had been searched. It was dangerous for me to leave the house because I would have been spotted as a stranger right away.

The Americans liberated the area on August 22nd,1944. Mme Merlette was advised to take me to the American Headquarters at Sens which she did. That was where I was interrogated by my own side.

The American officer who interviewed me couldn't understand me at all. I had no proof of identification. The Germans had taken both my identity discs away when I had been wounded and I didn't have the speech to tell him who I was or what had happened. I made noises and signs. It wasn't long before he was convinced that I was a German acting up, pretending to be English. I was put in a prisoner of war cage along with German prisoners. Luckily, one of the men from the Resistance who had been in the forest where I had been shot saw me in there and shouted a greeting. He immediately informed the American officer in charge who I was. I was taken out of the cage straight away. Two officers contacted Praz who accompanied us to Sens Hospital where my identity was confirmed. I was seen by an American doctor and hospitalised. That was where I met three members of the Resistance that knew me. One of them was badly wounded. A few days later I received permission to return to Chaumont to say goodbye to M.and Mme Merlette. The following day in August 1944, I was flown back to England and spent four years in Wharncliffe Hospital, Wakefield and was discharged in 1948 with 100% disability pension.The L.N.E.R. were helpful and found a job for me in the office. That was the best thing that could ever have happened to me because that was where I met Marjorie.

As time went by, I began to remember more details of the time I had spent in France although it always troubled me that my memories were so sketchy and not in any sequence. I also had great difficulty in remembering names and places. Despite this, I never lost the feeling of gratitude for the many brave people who had risked their lives to help me, a severely wounded airman. In 1969, I contacted Mme Jeanne Gilliat, the French consul in Leeds, to ask for help to trace anyone who had helped me. The two key words I could recall were Sens and Mimi. A few months later, I received a letter from her with M. and Mme Merlotte's address. In 1970, we went to stay in Chaumont. As a result of local newspaper coverage, many people contacted us. At a reunion on the 19th of September, 1971, I was overjoyed to be able to meet and thank many of those courageous people who had saved my life almost thirty years before.

Jack Marsden

19th September 1971 - Re-union day at St Julien-du-Sault.

The lady with Jack is Madame Vautier one of the nurses who helped to give him medical aid whilst he was being sheltered - a very brave lady - one of the bravest ladies.
The man with the spotted tie is Le Sous-Préfet de Sens, also Flt. Lt. JR Summers.

• • • • • • •

I was eighteen and worked in the Goods Office of the L.N.E.R. at Dewsbury (West Yorkshire). The door opened and I looked up from my desk. This tall, fair haired man stood in the opening and I can remember thinking, "Wow."

I didn't know anything about him then but I can remember my reaction and recall his smile. He told us that he had come to say hello and that he would be coming to work with us because a job had been found for him which took account of his disabilities. That was in August 1948. Jack had spent the last four years in Wharncliffe Hospital.

It wasn't long before the two of us were going to the pictures together. He used to give me his sweet coupons because he preferred cigarettes, a habit which increased while he had been in hospital. Jack was six foot tall and the paralysis on his right side was still affecting him. He still walked with a limp. He never did regain normal feeling in that side. He also had problems with his speech, in fact he had to ask one of our colleagues to teach him how to pronounce my name.

Jack had a War pension but this was constantly reviewed. I went with him to the first of many Medical Board Examinations at Chapel Allerton in Leeds. He was receiving 100% War pension and he had that for the rest of his life.

It was a beautiful sunny day. Later we had a delicious meal of gammon, egg and chips at Sherwins Restaurant in Leeds and, in the evening, we went to the Empire theatre to see George Formby.

Unfortunately, the injury to his brain had left him suffering from epilepsy but, while he was in hospital, he had fallen through a plate glass window and his left hand had been badly cut and he had lost a lot of blood. This had left that hand virtually useless but his fits never seemed quite as bad after that. The part of his brain that had not been affected was the part dealing with figures and he was extremely good at that.

We got engaged at Christmas 1949. We married in December 1950 and our first daughter, Barbara, was born on 10 March, 1953. Our second daughter, Janet, was born on 7. November, 1954. We settled down to the family life that Jack had never expected to have and we were so happy together.

Jack never lost his sense of humour and never complained about his injuries.

He was able to work for 20 years but he was made redundant by Dr Beeching's drastic cuts to the railway network. We were really worried then and wondered how we would cope financially but, at the end of the day, we were only one pound a week worse off because our allowance for the girls was increased.

We were as happy then as we had ever been. We had more time together and Jack could spend more time in the garden. He loved gardening, particularly growing vegetables. We bought a green-house. He spent every minute he could in the garden and I would often have to shout up the garden and ask him if he wanted a candle to see where he was digging. He still had bad days but they didn't last for ever. He often used to sit down and say, "I feel as though I've been hit in the head by a donkey."

As the years went by, the epileptic fits that caused his accident at the hospital which had cut the tendons in his left hand became more controlled. His speech was slowly improving and he hoped and expected that his memory would return in the same way. He was so disappointed when that didn't happen because he knew there were so many people in France that had helped him and it troubled him that he couldn't remember their names. The injury to his brain had affected his memory and he couldn't remember the brave people who had allowed us to have the family life that we treasured. Then, in 1970, we managed to contact one of those wonderful people. All four of us went to a reunion in France in 1971 and we were made so welcome and, as we talked, so bits of the memories came back to him. There was one piece of the jigsaw that he never did know and that was where his plane had actually crashed. We discovered that it had landed at St Maurice aux Riches Hommes. We

Return visit to 'Le Oasis in 1972

went there to meet the farmer. He had been seven years of age at the time of the raid and he had hidden under the table but he told us how a burning wheel from the Lancaster had spun across the fields like a Catherine wheel. We walked round the field and were amazed to pick up pieces of the plane that were still scattered across the field.

In spite of all the hardships he had to endure since being so severely wounded when he was only 19 years old, Jack kept smiling and never lost his sense of humour. He set me a fine example. Jack died in 1976 and I was devastated despite having the loving support of my family. I still miss him. It is his courage and inspiration which has allowed me to rebuild a life of quality just as he had to.

Marjorie Marsden.

The crew of Lancaster LL 743 of 166 Squadron was shot down over Mailly le Camp and Sergeant Sanderson ordered the crew to bail out. He himslf was badly burnt but was found and helped by local people and taken to Mme Duquesne at Troyes where he stayed for a short while before being taken to Loines aux Bois where he was sheltered by Mme Patris. He was discovered by the Germans and both he and Mme Patris were arrested. Sergeant Sanderson became a P.O.W. (prisoner of war) and Mme Patris was sent to a concentration camp. She died in the train en route for the camp on July 2nd. 1944.

· · · · · · ·

It seemed like a good idea at the time. I was in a reserved occupation when war broke out, working in a local iron foundry. I watched my pals go off one by one to join up and knew the excitement of the war. A close friend and myself resolved to volunteer but we were turned away because, "we are full up at the moment." John and I then went to Glasgow and we joined up there. He was accepted for the marines, I for the R.A.F. I never saw him again.

Now, on May 3rd. 1944 and some dozen missions later, we awaited another routine briefing. Nothing special was anticipated. It never was. We were on stand by and had lazed the morning away waiting for the afternoon briefing. Our crew had been together throughout almost all of the missions we had completed and tended to do everything together during our off duty time as well. We were a mixed bag of people but over these years had come to rely very heavily on each other in the air and that created a bond that was to last throughout our lives.

It was late morning when the briefing was called. Security was very tight. There was the usual anticipation of the string drawing out the route to the target. It was a short string. It looked like another short, easy mission.

Then the Intelligence Officer introduced the reality, Mailly, a huge military camp. Information had been sent by the Resistance and it had to be destroyed. It was essential. Details followed of Mailly's function as a gathering and servicing centre for German Panzer Divisions. This was seen as crucial to repulse an allied invasion in Northern Europe. It had to be removed from Operational use.

The penny dropped. It was just another raid but this one really mattered.

Briefing continued. There were three main targets. Group Captain Cheshire's Pathfinders were to mark the target area with flares, more detailed marking than usual. Second stage briefings were for individual groups: pilots, Gunners, Navigators, bomb aimers, radio operators and engineers. Then it was personal preparations, parachutes, letters, shaving and, the special treat, an egg with our bacon.

We were driven out to the dispersal area and killed a bit of time with idle chat. Ginger ran a final engine check and we were ready for the off. It was 23.00 hours, time to go.

It was a clear night and visibility was superb. Charles started us rolling and the raid was on. The route was not direct. Defence installations in North West France were well known and our route was a course avoiding them. We had window on board, silver strips which filled the enemy radar screens with snow storms and we dropped this at regular intervals. Our Canadian navigator, Tug, had a fairly straightforward bit of work ahead of him, at least on the outward run. We headed for the collection area above Challons to wait for the order to attack when the Pathfinders had marked the target.

It was all quiet as we approached Challons. Mac had imposed RT silence to keep the air clear so that he could receive the signal to go in and bomb. Everything was quiet. There was no ack ack guns, no German fighters. We started to circle above Challons. We circled again and again and again. There was no message.

There was no radio silence either. There were American voices and Glenn Miller music. It was the Germans trying to jam our communications or so we thought. Whatever the reason, our contact with the Pathfinders and the Master Bomber was broken.

Outside, hell had broken out. German night fighters had arrived in force and were attacking the circling bombers. Lancaster down... ....and another........and another.........two fly into each other and explode in the air and others scatter so that they are not hit by the debris. And still there was no attack order. Stan, the mid upper gunner, and I kept our eyes open but no fighter attacked us. There were plenty of other targets.

Suddenly RT was broken by a strong Aussie voice. "The hell with this, let's go before we're picked off." And go we did. Charles lined us up for a clear run in and Nick dropped his bombs right on target and we made a bee line for home without further incident but going like hell.

We landed safely and went straight to debriefing. We were safely home and glad to be so. Good mission, we thought, or was it? The truth of the losses was beginning to come in - 42 crews lost The radio jamming had caused the delay and the circling Lancasters had been easy prey for the German fighters.

It was time for us to relax, time for another treat, another egg and bacon. Time to relax but never to forget.

Jimmy Graham

> Jimmy Graham was a member of the crew of Q for Queenie of
> 576 Squadron based at Elsham Wolds on the night of the Mailly
> le Camp raid, 3rd-4th of May 1944.

· · · · · · ·

I was a flight sergeant rear gunner on a Lancaster. I was in a Squadron stationed at Spilsby in Lincolnshire. I'd joined up when I was seventeen and a half and volunteered for air crew. All air crew were volunteers. There was one thing you learned in the forces and that was to get on with all types of people but this was particularly true of the crew on a Lanc. They became your second family. There was one man who had been a gamekeeper and he lived in the woods between raids. He was a good crew member but he preferred the fresh air. He built himself a tree house and slept there even in the depths of winter.

If you weren't alive in the war, I suppose you'll find it difficult

to understand the atmosphere that existed or the sense of humour amongst the troops.

It was forbidden to have brothers in the same squadron but the Aussies always found ways of ignoring the rules. We had two pairs of New Zealand brothers on our strength. We'd just returned from a raid one day and I was walking behind an Aussie when the C.O. came across and put his hand on his shoulder.

"I'm sorry, Dave," he said, "but your brother's plane has bought it. There are witnesses who saw it explode in the air. I'm afraid there were no survivors."

"That's alright, Sir, " Dave said, "I'll have his egg and bacon."

There was a feeling of excitement and adventure and determination and, as soon as you donned a uniform, you became part of it. There was a tension at times but you learned to live with it. You had to. You got used to this constant movement of men as they were posted to other stations, except for your own crew. Once we had been formed as a crew, we stayed together. Death was part of the scene and you'd feel a sense of sorrow when a certain crew had not returned but then you got on with the job. You never thought that one day you could be the one that didn't return. It always happened to the other man.

As soon as we were over the coast, we could expect tracer fire and flak. The experienced pilots jinxed to avoid enemy fighters and tried to use cloud cover so that they couldn't be picked up by searchlights. It was the clear, moonlight nights we feared when the planes would leave *vapour trails across the sky.*

We went on some long raids. A trip to Turin, for example, was ten and a half hours in the air and we had to stay alert for every second of it. When a fighter approached, I would only have it in my sight for a matter of seconds and that was my only chance to shoot at it.

I had completed one tour (30 raids) and was on my second when we went on the raid to Mailly le Camp. It was a disaster from start to finish and anyone else who was on that raid will tell you the same. We found out afterwards that the radio had failed but we didn't know that then. We were circling round waiting for the order to go in and drop our bombs. We were like sitting ducks in full view of the enemy because it was one of those clear, moonlit nights that we dreaded.

42 planes failed to return from that raid and we were one of them. We were hit by light flak on the port wing and began to lose fuel although we weren't aware of it at the time. Then we had three attacks by Focke-Wulfe 190s and an ME 110 attacked us from below, aiming at our fuel tanks. That was a favourite trick of theirs. We were well on fire. My parachute was hanging in the fuselage. There hadn't been enough room to keep it in the turret with me. I had to turn the turret round, reach for my parachute, put it on, turn the turret round again and jump for it.

Only the parachute wasn't there when I reached for it. All the lights had gone out and I was crawling through thick, black, choking smoke feeling for it. I was lucky. It was one of the luckiest moments of my life. I put my hand right on it. It had broken loose and was rolling about on the floor. I put it on and made for the rear door. Just before I jumped, I picked up the intercom and told the pilot I was leaving.

"I thought you'd gone already, you curly, black headed bastard," he said but his words didn't come easily. I could hear him gasping as he fought to control the plane steady long enough for us all to escape. They were probably the last words he spoke.

I had to jump through flames. The engines were well alight and there was no way I could avoid them. I didn't open my parachute until I had cleared it. Within seconds of my leaving the plane, one of the wings broke off and went over my head. It was so close that I could see every detail on it. I can remember looking up at the plane and noting that the propellors were still going round. It was as I looked up that I realised two panels of my parachute were on fire and the flames were spreading rapidly.. I was falling faster and faster. I fell rather

*than floated and landed in a ploughed field. I was dropping so fast
that I went into the earth up to my knees. I released myself from the
parachute and lay there. I knew I had been burned, mostly on my head
and across my shoulders. But it was my eyes that were the problem. I
lay there and didn't know what to do. I heard someone coming towards
me.*

"Kamarade," I said.

*"You silly b., "a voice answered with a broad Yorkshire accent.
"It's me, Jack." Jack was the navigator. "Come on, we've got to get
moving."*

*We gathered up our parachutes so that if the Germans came they
wouldn't know that there had been any survivors. Then we started
walking. I had both hands on Jack's shoulders and he was telling
me where we were going. We found a derelict cottage and stuffed the
parachutes up the chimney. Then we crossed a road. We were half
way across it when we heard trucks coming towards us. Jack pulled
me after him and we made for the other side of the road and tumbled
into a ditch. It was deeper than we thought with a foot of water in
the bottom. The trucks pulled up right alongside us. We hardly dared
breathe let alone move.*

*Orders were given to the German troops from the trucks. They
spread out along the road and started walking towards the burning
plane. They obviously thought there were no survivors because they
came back to the trucks quite quickly and drove off. We waited for
a few minutes and then climbed out of the ditch and started walking
down the road. I relied on Jack to lead me and explain where we were
going. We had our uniforms on and our flying boots so there was no
denying who we were. We reached a village and walked right along*

the main road. It was about six o'clock by this time and people were beginning to move. The baker was standing in front of his shop. A couple of other people stood and stared at us. Nobody said anything or tried to stop us. We went into a cemetry and found shelter in a big, old family tomb and we settled down there. That was when the pain hit me and it got worse and worse until I became delirious. The vault in which we were hiding was against a wall and an elderly couple were tending their garden on the other side of the wall. They must have realised we were there but they carried on gardening as if there was nothing amiss.

As evening fell, two French men came to our hiding place. Jack was fit and they told me that they were going to take Jack with them and that they would be back to see to me later. I know now that they thought I would die in the night and that the old couple on the other side of the wall dug a hole beneath their vines because they thought that they would have to bury me.

Two men from the underground came back early the next morning and, when they saw I was still alive, they fetched a doctor to look at me. He said that I needed specialist treatment and they should take me to the next village where there was a surgeon who specialised in burns and had recently returned from Paris to take over his father's practice. The men contacted him and he came and fetched me and took me to his own home and looked after me for six weeks. It is impossible for me to put into words the feelings I have for these brave people. I wouldn't be here today if it hadn't been for them.

I couldn't have been in better care than I was in the doctor's home. As I got better I began to worry about the risk my presence there was imposing on him and his family. The problem was that medicine was difficult to obtain. He needed sulphanilamide to treat me. The local Maquis sent a message to London asking for the drug and explaining why it was needed. Two days later, there was a knock on the door and a parcel addressed to Flight Sergeant Emeny was handed over. It contained not sulphamilamide but penicillin.. I found out later that a pilot called Martin Verity had flown over in a Lysander to deliver it. I had never heard of penicillin, neither had the doctor. He did not know what the dosage was or how much to give me. It was a hit and miss affair but it did the trick. I started to improve straight away.

I stayed with the doctor for six weeks until I was considered fit enough to move to Paris. I was given French clothes that fitted me as if they had been made for me. My head was still bandaged but I could see again. The doctor had been bathing my eyes each day and it was a wonderful moment when he told me that my eyes had not been burned.

A fifteen year old boy took me to Paris. When we reached the station he told me that he couldn't come any further. A lady with two bikes would be waiting outside the station. One of the bikes was for me. It was important that he did not see her because, then, if he was ever caught, he would not be able to identify her.

Sure enough, the lady was waiting. She asked me in perfect English if I could ride a bike. It turned out that she was American and had been caught in Paris when the Americans came into the war. She asked me where I came from and I told her London.

"We have another man from London," she said, "perhaps you'll know him."

"Oh yes," I thought.

We reached a block of flats and, leaving our bikes in the entrance, we climbed to the top floor, the fifth. She opened the door and showed me into a small room in her flat.

"Hello Ron," a voice said and there, sitting on the floor with his feet towards the centre of the room was Len Barnes, the boy who had sat next to me at school. "It's a pity you weren't here yesterday," he went on, "you'd have met Reg Lewis. He was here."
Reg had been in our class as well.

There were fourteen of us in that room. There was not enough room to lie down. We had to sit with our feet towards the centre of the room and we had to keep quiet. We could not let any of the other people who lived in that block of flats have any idea that we were there. The worst thing was the toilet. We couldn't keep pulling the chain. That could have given the game away. We could only pull it five or six times.

We had been there for a few days when Madame Virginia, as we called her, told us that arrangements had been made to get our identity cards but first of all, we had to have our photos taken. We were to leave the flat two at a time and meet outside where bikes would be waiting for us. Sure enough everything worked as she said and we set off in a long line with Madame Virginia leading us and her husband bringing up the rear. We went round the Arc de Triomphe, down La Place de la Concorde to the Boulevard Sebastapol. There we went in two at a time to have our photographs taken.

50

That evening five of us left for Bordeaux, three Americans, Len and myself. We made our way across Paris by Metro to the Gare d'Ouest. We got on the train without any trouble. We had the correct tickets and our papers were all in order. Mine said that I was a deaf mute. I was on my own but I knew the others weren't far away. Germans occupied all the carriages, lying along the seats so that there wasn't room for anyone else. I stood in the corridor but I was aware that Len was standing at the other end and I knew the Americans were further up the train.

We left at six o'clock in the morning and arrived at Bordeaux at six the following morning. The train kept stopping. There were air raids in progress throughout the night and it felt strange being on the receiving end for once.. Every so often, we would pull into a siding and the engine would be changed. Allied bombers had destroyed so much that the French were having trouble keeping the trains running. We had to spend the day in Bordeaux. Our train to Biarritz was not leaving until the evening so Michou, the young French girl who was guiding us, took us down to a park and told us to spend the day there. It was very relaxing in the park. Michou returned at mid-day with sandwiches and a flask of coffee. We were happy sitting there chattering when Michou returned in an agitated state and told us to get out of the park quickly. We almost ran after her. We got out of the gates and spread out along the road and started to walk away casually just as German army lorries roared up to the park gates. We carried on walking as the soldiers locked the park gates and started searching.

I think we were all relieved when we boarded the Biarritz train. We were spread out in the same way that we had been on the train from Paris. We were travelling through a forbidden zone and I was feeling tense. We were getting close to the Spanish border and caught our first sight of the Pyrenees. We knew our passes were in order but it was still a funny feeling as we drew nearer and nearer to the mountains, part excitement but also a heightened awareness of the dangers that still surrounded us.

There were two Germans in the carriage, to start with they slept peacefully. Then they woke up and started to move around. They came out into the corridor and one of them demanded a light for his cigarette. I told them, "pas de fumeur," but they wouldn't take no for an answer and started to jostle me. I didn't know what to do. I knew I mustn't do anything that would draw attention to myself. If

51

they found out that I was a British airman, then they would catch all five of us because it was well known that people trying to escape over the Pyrenees travelled in small groups and they would also know that there was a member of the French resistance travelling with us.

At that moment the train drew into a small country station and I got off,. At this point the road ran along beside the railway so I simply started walking. The train pulled out of the station and I saw Len's face looking out with consternation. He hadn't seen what had been happening with the Germans.

I left the village and carried on walking along the road. There was an old man working in his garden and he called out, "M'sieur, m'sieur, English soldat?"

I told him I was an airman.

"You walk like a soldier," he told me.

He had fought alongside English troops in the First World War, so he had a little English. He stood behind me and bent my shoulders forward so that I slouched. He pushed my hands into my pockets and pulled my beret over my forehead. "Now you walk like a Frenchman," he said.

I carried on walking. I must have been walking for an hour when two men approached on bicycles pulling another one between them. They started riding round me in a circle when they reached me without saying anything. Then one of them asked, "English aviator?"

I said I was and one of them indicated the spare bike. We cycled into Biarritz and round to a café where the others were waiting. We stayed there until it was time for us to take a tram for Sibour, a little village at the foot of the mountains. It was more like a train than a tram. It ran on rails but it had a conductor and kept stopping like a tram. Michou, our guide, was still with us and explained that we would have to cross the River Bidoser by a bridge that would be guarded. She told us to walk as normally as possible and the guards would not stop us. We did and they didn't but it was a tense moment.

Michou took us to a little Basque hovel with mud floors and a room in the roof. There were already donkeys, pigs and hens sheltering in the place as well as the six men that had left the flat in Paris a few days before us. We settled down with them in the hay. It was alive and it wasn't long before we were too. We had only been there a short time when Florentine appeared at the door and said, "We go." The six men who had been waiting went straight away. Two days later, it was our turn. *Florentine had come back for us.*

He was one of the most powerful and purposeful men I had ever met. He had led many allied people over the mountains. I'm not the only person who owes a lot to him.

We followed him up the tracks and it was strenuous. We hadn't had much exercise over the last few weeks and we found it hard going. We had been moving for ten and a half hours when he called a halt. It was cold, bitterly cold. It had been pleasantly warm in Biarritz but now we were on the snowline. Florentine told us to wait there while he went for food. He didn't come back. We waited for a long time. It had started to rain and the rain grew steadily heavier. We could see the glow of lights from the Spanish town and we decided that we couldn't wait any longer. We would go on on our own. At times the rain was so heavy that it was difficult to see where we were going. We were soaked through but we were beginning to go down and we could see the lights of Spain through the curtain of rain. Then we saw some sheds and, much to our surprise, there were people living in them, two shepherds, a woman and two children. They had nothing. There was no food and they were dressed in rags. They signalled for us to shelter from the rain and we were pleased to get under cover. They started talking amongst themselves. Then one of the shepherds signalled that he was leaving. One of the Americans spoke Spanish. He'd picked up a bit of the language when he had traded with Puerto Rica before the war. He said it was time for us to go as well. The man who had left had told the others to keep us there. He'd obviously gone for the Germans and was looking for a reward. The other peasants tried to keep us there but we pushed them out of the way and carried on walking.

The rain stopped in the morning so we rested for a while and dried out. We had no food but there was plenty of water. It was ice cold and those of us that had fillings in our teeth were soon reminded of them.

It was early in the morning that we caught sight of the Spanish town and we made for it. We found out later that it was Pamplona. Half way down the mountain, we came across a young man sitting on a rock. He had a hand of bananas and a skin of wine. He was Florentino's son and had been waiting there for us for three days. That was how we found out that Florentino had been shot in the legs by some Germans. His son had come into the mountains looking for us. He had met up with the shepherds who had told him that we had passed so he thought it was best that he waited at that point We had not eaten for days and those bananas were good, so was the wine. We were in much better spirits when we made for the town.

The young man explained that he was going to hand us over to the police because the Gestapo kept watch on the British consul and there had been instances where they had kidnapped some of the airmen that had been rescued so we would be kept at the Spanish police station until someone from our Consul came and collected us.

It was filthy. The first thing that happened to us when we reached the police station was that we were deloused. Then we were put in a cell and locked up. The other six who had been with us in Paris were already there. There was straw on the floor but, at least, we felt cleaner until the others pointed at the ceiling. There were these bugs, fully three inches long clinging to the wall above us. "You wait until it gets dark and they come looking for warmth," the others told us.

We'd been in this cell for a couple of days when there was this hell of a commotion and this Spanish officer arrived. He had so much gold braid on his uniform it was a wonder he wasn't weighed down by it. He assembled the Spaniards together and spoke to them for a long time without pausing for breath. Willy translated for us. It seemed that the allies had landed in Normandy and, despite all the German talk, they were falling back and the allies were advancing steadily. The men were told that they better look after us. A few hours later, we were transferred to a hotel but, first of all, the Spanish officer asked us to write something to say that we had been well treated. One of the Americans fancied himself as a writer and took a lot of care in writing out a certificate.

"This Officer is a bastard and should be shot at sight."

When he went back to Spain several years after the war, he found the officer sitting at his desk with that same certificate framed and hanging on the wall behind him.

There were baths at the hotel and clean clothes for us. They asked if we would like an English breakfast and we said, "Yes please." They brought in bowls of fresh fruit, then they brought in a big bowl of eggs swimming in olive oil and lumps of bacon in another dish also swimming in olive oil. We gave it to the children that had gathered round us. We ate the fruit.

We then had an escort from the Spanish airforce and he took us to Irun by train. We were taken to a really smart hotel there. About mid-day the following morning, a Rolls Royce arrived at the front of the hotel. The chauffeur leapt out and opened the back door and out stepped a man about our own age resplendent in a pin striped suit, a bowler hat and a rolled umbrella. He wandered into the foyer.

"Who are the R.A.F. chappies?" he asked.

As soon as we had identified ourselves, he told us to jump into the jolly old Rolls.

"What about us?" the Americans asked.

"Oh, I expect they'll send a jeep for you," the young man answered.

We went to the Embassy but the consul didn't appreciate our presence.

"I do wish you R.A.F. chappies would stop walking over the jolly old mountains," he started when he saw us. "It makes it so embarrassing for me. I get pinholed by the German Ambassador about you all every time I go to a cocktail party or dinner."

He really cut us down to size. We complained about him when we got back to England and he was replaced.

We were given money and papers and put in the care of the Spanish Airforce. We travelled to Saragossa by train. This was in the middle of Franco's country and was where the Headquarters of the Condor Regiment was situated. The Spanish officers were keen to get rid of us. Spain had been a neutral country during the war but many Spaniards supported the Germans especially as they had fought alongside them during their own Civil War. The Spanish regiment that had fought with the S.S. in Russia had returned and there was to be a march through the streets to celebrate their return. The Officers thought it would be best if we were out of the town when that took place and we were taken up into the hills, to the spa town of Alamah de Arrogon. There were two hotels there, one occupied by the Americans and the other by the British and they were luxurious. I had my own room and bathroom. When I looked in the cupboards, I found that they were packed with clothes and we were told to help ourselves to them. Well, I kitted myself out. Clothes were rationed in Britain. It would be a long time before I had an opportunity like that. I selected a suit, shirts, underclothes, socks, shoes, the lot and so did the others.

We were picked up by the British sub consul. He was a different kind of man to the other two we had met from the Embassy. He was friendly but efficient, the sort of man that you didn't argue with. He took us to the home of Mr Williams of the firm Williams and Humbert. He owned a sherry factory. He gave us a tour of it and presented each of us with a bottle of presentation sherry that had been bottled for the coronation of Edward in 1937. As he had never been crowned the sherry had remained on the shelf. We stayed with Mr Williams for two days and then we were collected by army lorry and taken to Gibraltar. The first thing we did when we got there was to go and buy cheap cases to carry all the clothes we had acquired. We were kitted out with uniforms in Gibraltar and put on a Dakota for home. We opened our bottles of sherry and drank them on the return journey except for Len. He kept his and sold it at an auction a couple of years later and got two thousand pounds for it. That was enough to buy a house in those days.

We landed at Bristol and were taken to the station for a train to London. It was while we were on the platform that we were mobbed.. Len and I had taken a hand of bananas home for our families. People in Britain hadn't seen a banana during the war and the children didn't know what they were. They tried to eat them with the skins on when we gave them some. It was the same on the train and in London. By the time we reached Marylebone, Len and I just had the stalks.

We were interrogated by Airey Neave from ten o'clock in the morning until four o'clock in the afternoon. Then he said that we might as well go home and go back in the morning. Len and I only lived a penny halfpenny tram journey away. We got off the tram outside the Crosskeys and decided we would pop in for a quick pint before we went home. There was such a shout when we went in.

"What are you doing here? We thought you were dead."

We had a quick drink and went home. My mother opened the door, took one look at me and fainted. They didn't even know we were still alive. They had had a telegram saying that I was missing believed killed and that was all they had heard. We took the matter up with Airey Neave the next day. He apologized and said that he shouldn't have let us go home. They didn't inform the families until the last minute in case there was a hold up on the journey.

I was posted to Coningsby, to the Pathfinder force. I wasn't allowed to fly over France until the allies had reached the Rhine. The problem was that I couldn't wear a helmet. The burns on my head hadn't healed as well as I thought, so I was sent to East Grinstead and became one of McIndoe's boys, the great plastic surgeon who worked such marvels on damaged and burned features.

I stayed in the R.A.F. and retrained as a wireless operator. I flew

Valiants and Vulcans. Twenty years after the war, I visited a U.S. Air base and one of the men mentioned the C.O., Lt. Colonel Hubberd.

"Just get a message to him and tell him that there's someone here who wants to know how the most expensive washer upper in Paris is getting on."

He said he couldn't do that but he did get a message to him when I told him what it was all about. He was one of the senior American officers who had always done the washing up in the Paris flat.

Then an announcement was made over the tannoy, "Gentlemen, smarten yourselves up, the C.O. is coming over," and there was Speedy at the top of the steps.

"You curly headed b....," his voice boomed out

I met the other Paris washer upper, Colonel Don Wallis at another U.S.A.F. base later on. We just stood and stared at each other. I can't remember which of us spoke first.

The third American, Jack Cordell, had been a man in torment in Paris. His aeroplane had been shot down and he was the only survivor. When he reached Spain, he had been sent straight back to America and spent the rest of his life in the Veterans Hospital in Washington.

Ron Emeny.

• • • • • • •

Pilot T. Blackman escaped from his aircraft, LM 480 of 50 squadron when it was shot down. Five members of his crew were killed. After hiding from the Germans, he met up with and joined the Resistance. He was eventually caught and sent to Buchenwald Concentration Camp.

• • • • • • •

I was a wireless operator stationed at Elsham Wolds in North Lincolnshire overlooking the Humber and it was cold. There was nothing between us and Russia and that was where the winds came from. It was a good station. There was a happy atmosphere at Elsham Wolds but we all knew we had a job to do and we did it. The spirit of cooperation and comradeship was terrific.

We were called in for briefing on the afternoon of May 3rd. 1944 and I think we were all relieved when the covers were taken off the maps and we saw that our target was in France. We had had some horrific operations to Germany. France was considered an easy option so much so that the powers that be had decided that raids to France only merited a third of a mission. We had to make three French raids to one over Germany. Thirty missions made up a tour and then we would generally go on leave or be posted to another station.

The target and route was explained to us at the briefing together with the details of the bomb load we were carrying and the weather conditions we could expect en route.. We were told it would be a piece of cake and we believed it..

There was always a sense of tension, a tightness when there was going to be a raid which was quite different to the days when no raid had been announced. Then there would be a rush to get ready for a night on the town. There wasn't the usual tension on May 3rd. We didn't expect any trouble. We went for our operational meal, then returned to our billets to get ready. Some of the men were superstitious and would go through a set pattern of behaviour before we went on a raid. Others would have a lucky mascot which was important to them. I just got myself ready and joined up with the rest of the crew. In a way, the crew were family. A close relationship had developed between us. We were so used to working together that we hated it if one of the crew was sick and we had someone we didn't know in his place. On this particular raid, we had a new plane and a new rear gunner, Bert Buckman.

We would get on one of the crew buses to be taken out to the plane. This was generally driven by the same W.A.A.F. The ground crew would be waiting for us and, again, they were the same men. They were part of our team. The captain would make the checks, sign the forms and signal us on board. We settled down on the plane. Every one of us knew our jobs and we got on with them. We worked as a unit.

Then the engines would turn over and we would feel the power of the Lanc. We taxied to the end of the runway and took off, one plane in a line of others.

As a radio operator, my job was to listen out for instructions and pass them on to the captain. We had to maintain radio silence because enemy fighters could pick up our transmissions and locate our position. I would keep tuned in so that I could hear instructions from the lead bomber. We had an internal system on the plane and we would chatter to each other because the radio system within the plane could not be picked up by the enemy. As we approached the target, a silence would fall over the plane, partly from the need to concentrate on our own specific jobs and partly from wondering what lay ahead of us.

We flew out over High Wycombe and across the Channel to France. It was a bright moonlit night, so bright that we could clearly see the countryside beneath us. Red flares had been dropped some twenty miles from Mailly to tell us that we were on the right route. As we approached the target, we could see it lit up and we knew that the first group had done their job. It was so bright that we didn't need the navigator to guide us in. We had maintained radio silence but, when I switched to the frequency to get our instructions, I could only hear the American forces' news broadcast and a lot of other garbled messages. We knew that Churchill had insisted that no French lives were to be lost on the raid and that the leaders were taking extreme care but we couldn't understand what was happening. They now think that the problems with the radios was caused by German jamming. We began to circle fifteen miles from Mailly waiting to be called in. The sky seemed to be full of circling Lancasters and there was a real fear that we would touch another plane.

Fred Browning was our pilot. "To hell with this," he said, "it's like moths caught in a candle," and he flew on and started circling thirty miles away.

We were called in to bomb at 12.32 hours. We should have bombed at 12.15. Those extra minutes were disastrous for so many crews. It gave the Germans time to muster their forces and there were four night fighter stations within reach. Their fighters were waiting for us when we returned. So were the searchlights, not that they were really needed. The moon was a better light and there was no escaping from it. I saw two Lancasters going down with smoke trails behind them.

Jack Spark - 60years on at East Kirkby

We were preparing for our bombing run when we heard a man screaming. It's a sound I will never forget. It frightened me to death. Then this cold, commanding voice broke in. "If you must die, die like a man," it ordered. It was more shocking than the scream.

Then we went in on the bombing run. The bomb aimer took over the plane. We had hardly got into position when another Lanc, twenty feet above us pressed the bomb release. Our gunner shouted out, "For God's sake, duck." It all happened too quickly for us to realise what a lucky escape we had had. As we turned for home, another plane exploded in the air. It was mayhem. We were one of the last planes to return to Elsham and, although our ground crew were pleased to see us, there was a subdued air in the camp.

They had said that raids over France only counted for a third of a mission but Mailly le Camp changed that. From then on, raids over France counted as a full mission. That meant we had done thirty operations. We had finished our tour. We had lived and flown as a crew and become close and important to each other. Now we simply said goodbye and went our own way. I became an instructor.

Jack Spark D.F.M.

• • • • • • •

I always reckoned that we were the luckiest crew in the squadron. We flew 34 missions and only had trouble on two of them, Essen and Mailly-le-Camp.

We lost an engine before we reached Essen and another over the target when we were attacked by a German night fighter. All I could think about was getting the crew home. The rest of the bomber crews had left us behind and we had the skies to ourselves but the Lancaster flew steadily on. As we approached the English coast two mosquitoes flew out and accompanied us in. We landed at West Malling in Kent.

Charles Wearmouth - President of the Elsham Wolds Association

The CO phoned Elsham Wolds to say we were safe and he was told to send us home by rail so we were given travel warrants and taken down to the station. We were in full flying kit, boots, helmets, parachutes, the lot and not a soul took any notice of us. We got to King' Cross and a lady porter came over and said, "I'll give you a hand with your luggage," and she picked up a parachute by its handle and immediately the parachute was fully open and towing the porter down the platform.

It was as we flew over Mailly le Camp that the same feeling of disaster we had experienced at Essen came to mind. I saw the Lancasters circling over the datum point and I knew they were asking for trouble. It was absolute mayhem. We flew straight on several

61

miles out from Mailly. I waited for the order to go in and bomb but all we could hear was Glen Miller and his music - The American Forces Radio. Then we heard the order to go in. The navigator gave us a course that took us straight in over the target. We dropped our bombs and flew straight on and home. We didn't see any German fighters and we weren't attacked but we saw aeroplanes that were. Two Lancasters exploded alongside us, another was diving towards the ground leaving a trail of smoke. Two parachutes emerged before it too exploded. We could see broken aircraft, flames and smoke, so much smoke. It wasn't until we were being debriefed that we realised how disastrous the raid had been.

Sqn Ldr Charles Wearmouth D.F.C. Pilot

• • • • • • •

We didn't see the night fighter that attacked us, there was this explosion and my panel had disappeared and a fire was burning and it was obvious it was out of control. The order came straight away to bale out. I wasn't the sort to panic but it was difficult not to in those circumstances. I kept repeating what I had to do, put on my parachute and make for the escape hatch. The bomb aimer went and I made to jump after him but I got caught up on the hatch. I couldn't free myself and it was getting hot. The Lanc was really burning. Then it gave a jolt and I was falling. The parachute opened and I was floating. It was like being in a dream. I got caught in a tree but I managed to get

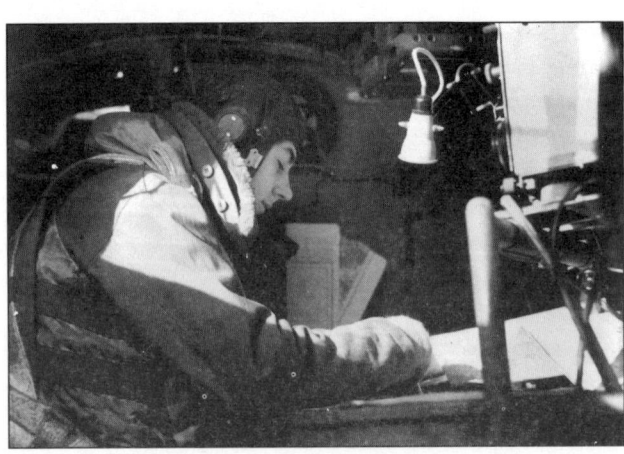

A navigator at work showing the cramped conditions inside the Lancaster

down to the ground but I couldn't stand. My legs couldn't support me. Then I heard whistling and the skipper was beside me. We waited until it was light and then we started to move but the skipper had to support me. He wouldn't leave me and try to make it on his own.

We were picked up by Germans and finished up as P.O.W.s (Prisoners of War). We were the only survivors from our crew. I couldn't understand that. I knew the bomb aimer and wireless operator had jumped before me. I've never found out what happened but they didn't make it.

L.C.T. Navigator

At first we thought the Germans were using scarecrows. That was a tactic we thought they had, firing flak into the air which descended as burning debris. We thought this was done to make us think they were shooting down our planes and this would affect our morale. Then we realised this was not a 'scarecrow'. It wasn't a hoax. It really was an aircraft burning on the ground.

M.T.

• • • • • • •

Flight Sergeant Godfery had parachuted to safety when his
aircraft was shot down, and sheltered in the home of Mme
Deguilly at Romilly sur Seine. He joined and fought with the
Resistance but the group was attacked by the Germans.

Sergeant Godfery was never seen again and nothing is known
of his fate.

• • • • • • •

*Imagine the scene, two scruffy crews arriving late at 101 Squadron,
Lufford Magna to face an irate C.O. Carey Foster.*

*"Oh my God, what have they sent me now," were his first words to
us, "more of Hitler's gun fodder?"*

*After a short, sharp lecture where he finished by saying that if we
played ball with him, he would play ball with us, he dismissed us.*

*The two crews shared a Nissen hut and we became good friends.
Mind you there was a lot of rivalry between us but it was good
humoured rivalry.*

*We were known as Bodger's and Whalley's. P.O. Bodger and
P.O.Whalley were the two pilots. Our bomb aimer was Sgt Barnes,
Sgt Lloyd was the engineer, I was the wireless operator air gunner
and Sergeants Robert and Russell were air gunners. Pilot Officer
Whalley's crew consisted of Sgt Vandervelde, engineer, F/Sgt Ward,
Navigator, F/Sgt Barr, Bomb aimer, F/Sgt Burgess, Wireless operator/
Air gunner, Sgt McCool and F/Sgt Reilly, air gunners.*

*We were in C flight and had completed seven operations when we
were told that we were being transferred to Elsham Wolds to combine
with a flight from 103 squadron to form 576 squadron. We had a better
reception at Elsham Wolds. We were treated as senior crews because
we had seven operations under our belts. The rivalry between our two
crews was intense, almost getting out of hand at times. We were at the
Oswald pub in Scunthorpe one night when the two crews challenged
each other. Whalley's crew was to take the barometer from the pub
while Bodger and crew were challenged to take the bell from the
station at Elsham Wolds. The pub landlord found out who had taken
the barometer and told Whalley that if it was returned he wouldn't say*

Ken Watkins and Jack Sparks

Ken Watkins (Centre) finally says goodbye to his comrades at Oeuilly 60 years on

any more about it. Unfortunately Whalley's crew couldn't remember where they had buried it, so Whalley was summoned and appeared in court. He was fined £5. It was in all the papers.

576's C.O. said he had a good idea who had taken the bell but, if it was back in its place by dinner time, nothing would be said, otherwise everyone on the station would be confined to camp. All was well. the bell was back in place by twelve o'clock.

Our crew had completed thirty missions but Ron Whalley's had only done twenty nine. They had one more to do, Mailly le Camp. Ron's parents had a pub in Islington and the two crews had planned a big party there when we had finished our tours. We decided to wait until they came back and we would travel down to London together, only they didn't come back. We waited until long after the last plane had landed. It was then that we heard that they had been shot down. We decided to go down to the pub. We had the sad task of telling Ron's parents. Even then, we didn't think they had been killed. They had been so much alive when they had set out on the raid. We told his mother that he had probably had to land at another airfield or they would have parachuted out. You didn't think of death, not when you had to face it so often, but I think we knew in our hearts that we wouldn't see them again. Life was there to be lived and we lived it.

We were posted then. It was ten years later, when I was at a reunion at Barnetby village hall and I met F/Sgt Vandervelde and F/Sgt Ward. I thought they had been killed when their plane crashed but it seemed they had baled out, hidden in a wood and then taken in by the Mayor of Oeuilly, the small village near the crash site. They were then taken to Spain by members of the French resistance and returned to England. It wasn't until 2002 that I discovered that Roy Whalley and his crew were buried in the little village churchyard at Oeuilly and told my family that I would like to go there. That was when we discovered that a coach was organised by John Burkett for the Elsham Wolds Association and was in contact with the Mailly association in France. It goes to Mailly le Camp every year. They were only too pleased to make arrangements with the Mayor of Oeuilly to visit the graves. How can I explain my feelings as I stood beside their graves and the bugler played the last post and in my mind I saw them laughing as they went out to their plane sixty years ago, shouting to us to be ready when they got back. There could not have been a more perfect or peaceful spot amongst that rolling countryside for me to say goodbye.

I shall always be grateful to the Mayor and people of Oeuilly for the welcome they gave me and for the care they take of the graves, to Mme Huguette Rouillard, to the colour party of 101 squadron and the R.A.F.A. colour bearer, Fred Mills and for so many who made it possible for me to make the journey to pay my last respects to such a fine group of young men. It was such an honour to have known them.

Ken Watkins. WOP/AG

· · · · · · ·

My brother was one of the airmen that failed to return from Mailly and all these years later, I still expect the gate to swing open and see him walking up the garden path with the grin on his face and his airforce cap tipped to one side. He loved the life in the Airforce and his crew was like a second family to him. Although I never met them, I felt I knew every one of them. There were three Johns in the crew and that made things difficult when they were on ops so my brother was known as F/Sgt Jack Bengston. He was the bomb aimer. Sgt John Maltby was known as Harry. He was the mid upper gunner and Sgt John Burgess, the engineer, kept his own name. Pilot Officer Douglas Wadsworth was the pilot

Sergeant Brady was the wireless operator. They flew a Lancaster Mark 3, JB 134 which they called Dirty Gertie. They had an eighth member of the crew that day, Arthur Naylor, a second bomb aimer. He was a German speaker and his job was to listen in for German fighter voice transmissions. Several Lancasters in 101 Squadron carried these special duties men from time to time. As soon as they located a signal, they would turn on a powerful transmitter, tune into it and flood it with interference. This was code named ABC – Airborne Cigar. The aeroplanes that used ABC had three, seven foot aerials attached to the airframe. It was thought that if a bomber transmitted messages, then German fighters could locate it. I don't know if that is what happened to my brother's plane but it was shot down by a German fighter.

Douglas Wadsworth was an experienced pilot and he managed to nurse the Lancaster over the village of Courboin before it crashed. They were all killed and are buried in the cemetry there.

Jim Bengston

●●●●●●●

Wednesday the third of May was a beautiful spring night, soft and starlit. We could see the shadows of the aircraft above us. They had been roaring over the village for a quarter of an hour when a torch of flame fell out of the sky. There was a terrific explosion and I was running towards it. I didn't have time to put on my shoes. What a sight met my eyes, a tangled mass of metal burning itself into the ground and the forest over which it had fallen was burning in a dozen places. The heat was intense. Black oily smoke rose in the sky and a pungent

smell filled the air. I looked up and saw the shadow of a plane flying low over us, a fighter come to check its kill. There was nothing I or anyone else could do.

We returned at day break. There was a huge crater in the middle of the meadow. Smoke and flames were still escaping from it. The ground all round it was burnt and tattered clothes were caught on the branches of the trees. I read the name Wadsworth on a piece of torn material. I wondered if that was a member of the crew or the name of the manufacturers of that particular garment. Other debris was strewn across the ground. It was complete devastation. There were lots of people about. My daughter picked up some partly burned French bank notes which she gave to the police when they arrived. A woman gave me an identity tag she had found. I put it carefully into my pocket. It carried the name H. Brady. R.A.F. 120.963. I wasn't going to let the Boche have that. There was nothing we could do. We stood around awed by the sight of the burnt plane.

Then the Boche arrived, five of them accompanied by three French policemen. The Germans were keen to know if the bomber had been shot down by a fighter but we wouldn't have said anything even if we had known. They soon made their report and left.

Our local policeman painstakingly collected the body parts. The village wheelwright made the coffin. They only needed one and on Friday, 5th May, the coffin was placed in the Chancel of the Church. It soon disappeared under a mountain of flowers.

We held the funeral the next day. The little Church was full to bursting filled by more than four hundred people. Two elderly ladies had walked ten kilometres to be there. I was one of the pall bearers. The man on my right was concerned because Fritz was in the village square. As the cortege passed through the square. a German officer stood to attention and saluted. Benedictions were said over the coffin at the cemetery and flowers piled on it. During the night, someone placed a Union Jack beside it.

I was arrested a month later. I had organised the funeral and I was under suspicion. I was taken to Paris and interrogated by the Nazis. They kept me there for three nights and then they released me. I was lucky but my name had been marked in red. I knew I had to be careful.

Monsieur M. L - village teacher - Courboin

• • • • • • •

I was a rear gunner on 103 Squadron flying out of Elsham Wolds. Mailly le Camp was my first raid and I was scared, I don't mind admitting it. I didn't know what to expect. There was a feeling of excitement mixed up with the fear but all other thoughts were pushed to the backs of our minds.

I can remember every second of that night and even as I'm talking to you, I have the picture of it all in my mind. I can see the men arriving from the briefing and they all looked so experienced without a care in the world and I remember the joking on the bus out to the aircraft. But the thing that really impressed me was the way the men gathered round their own Lancasters waiting for their captains to tell them to get on board. And I was one of them.

I can remember those captains too. They seemed so important yet most of them almost strolled round their aircraft as they did the final checks. There was Squadron Leader Jack Swanston with his cap pushed to the back of his head and Pilot officer Pat Furlong who always looked incredibly smart. Then there were three Flying Officers, Way, Leggett and Young who seemed to be great friends and a couple of Canadians, Pilot Officer Moore and Flight Sergeant Tate. You wouldn't have argued with those two. Pilot Officer Rowe was a typical Australian who didn't seem to have a care in the world and the

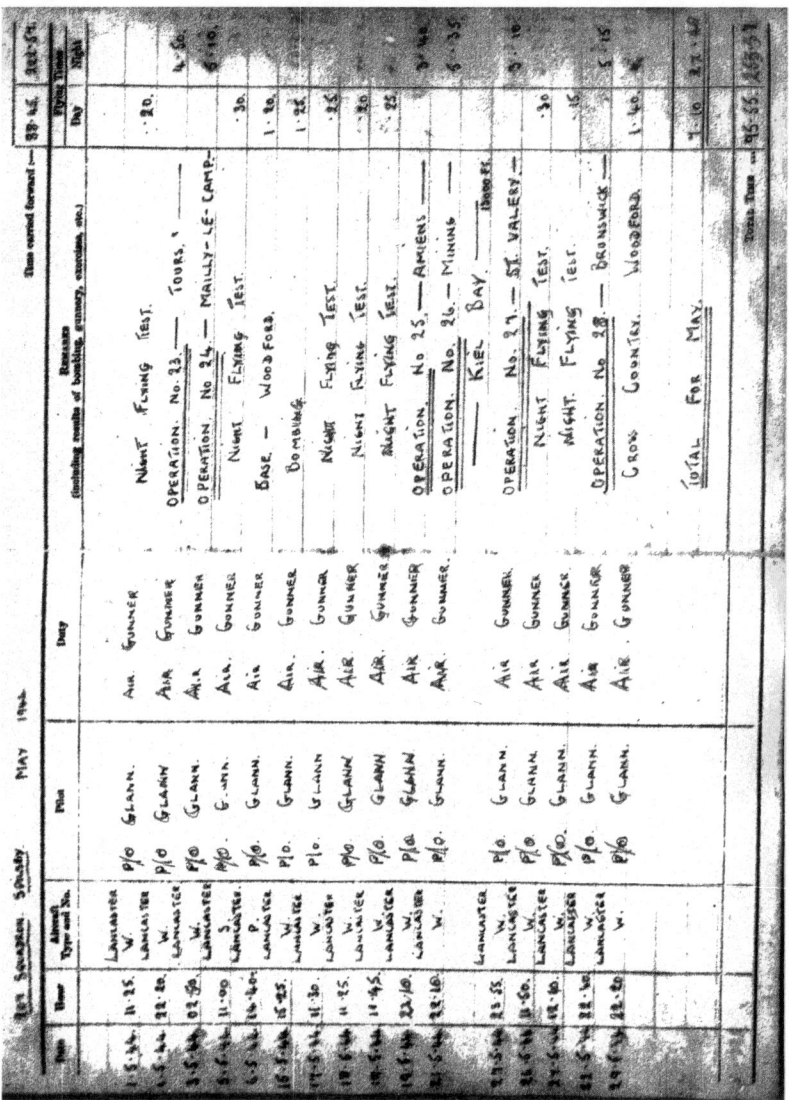

Aircrew Log Book

others that I can't remember too clearly, Flying Officers Broadbent, Armstrong and Morrison, Pilot Officer Whitley and Flight Sergeant Browning.

The life expectancy of a wartime pilot was 40 hours and that didn't do a lot for my confidence but it helped when we were airborne and I could see other Lancasters flying steadily behind us. The prospect of being left behind by the main stream was unnerving but fortunately that didn't happen to us, rather the reverse. There was a build up in the numbers over the marker and I could sense the tenseness from the skipper over the intercom. The Lanc climbed steeply at one point and I heard the exclamation, "That was close." But I couldn't see what was happening in front. I was a rear gunner, a tail end Charlie, and I could only see what was happening to the rear of us and that was plenty.

German night fighters were close and I was ready for them but they approached at such a speed that I would only see them for a matter of seconds in the target aimer before they were up and over us. I can remember a Messerschmitt coming at us with its guns firing. I fired at it as soon as I had it in my sights and it sprayed us with bullets but it didn't affect our flying luckily. I doubt if I saw the thing for more than five seconds. It all happened so quickly.

We came up to the target at 23,000 feet. The markers were visible. "Bomb doors open," the statement came over the intercom. Some flak was coming up at us and it was like riding a bike with flat tyres over cobble stones.

Jack stated, "Bombs gone."

Alec gave the course for out and the Skipper said, "Let's go home."

There was no flak. The gunners had left it open for their nightfighters to attack. I had a different view now and I looked back on a scene of absolute carnage. There were flames and smoke from the place we had bombed but there was also the sight of fallen and falling planes.

We made it home and I hardly had the strength to climb out of the plane. I was absolutely exhausted. I hadn't done anything to make me feel so tired but I suppose reaction had set in. We looked round the Lanc. It had been knocked about and it would need to be patched up before it flew again. We were all subdued as we went to the de-briefing. We took our coffee to the de-briefing table. It had a tot of rum in it. I didn't like rum. What the hell. We had got home and I was alive. It tasted good.

T.B. Rear gunner.

• • • • • • •

We hid under the table when the air raid started. I was seven years old and I was frightened. We'd heard the bombers flying over us for some time before the bombing started. Then this Lancaster crashed two fields over. It came in low over the house. I don't know how it missed us. When it hit the ground, it exploded and the burning wheel separated from the rest of debris and spun across the fields like a Catherine Wheel leaving a line of burning crops in its wake. We went out the next morning and there were fragments of metal all over the ground. There wasn't any piece that suggested it could have been an aeroplane. We're still ploughing up bits of that plane today. There was the remains of one airman in the plane and he was buried in the village cemetery.

Monsieur Le T. - Farmer

• • • • • • •

We flew out of Ludford Magna. I was a rear gunner on 101 Squadron. Our skipper was Flight Lieutenant Keard and our wireless operator/air gunner was Sergeant Crawford. Sergeant Webster was the flight engineer and Sergeant Spowart, the bomb aimer. Flying Officer Shannon was the navigator and Sergeant Clarence the mid upper gunner. There were three sets of Browning machine guns on a Lancaster, two on the front beneath the pilot's position and two in the roof. The mid upper gunner had a precarious position because his feet rested on a support similar to a rung on a ladder. He looked out of the plane through a small perspex dome so that he had a good view all round him. Then there were the guns to the rear of the plane and that was my domain.

Jack Worsford

We had an eighth member of the crew on board. Several of 101's Lancasters had this eighth member as part of a scheme code named

Jack Worsford's regular crew

Airborne Cigar (ABC) He was a German speaker and I was never sure why he was there. We didn't know him like we did the rest of the crew.

Setting off for Mailly le Camp was like setting off for any raid. Perhaps it was more relaxed because we didn't expect any trouble on a raid over France but the German night fighters were waiting for us and that was that. We were hit as we approached the target and we exploded in the air. The rear turret was blown right off. I can't really explain what it was like. I seemed to be in a haze. I knew I was falling but I wasn't frightened. It seemed to be happening to someone else. I think I thought of home but it was a long time ago now and I can't be sure. Then there was a jolt and I was shaken about for a few seconds and that was that. The only thing I could think about was the pain in my leg. It was almost unbearable. I managed to get out of my turret and found myself in a small wood. I hid up until the morning. Then I set to find help. The pain in my leg was so bad that I could hardly think.

I had landed at the village of Aubeterre which is near Mailly. As I started to walk across the field towards the village, I met a group of people who were coming to look at the debris of the plane. They were amazed to find me. They had seen the aircraft explode in the air and hadn't thought that there could have possibly been any survivors. They hadn't bothered to go out and look and they had only come out in the morning through curiosity. It seemed the plane had broken into three parts and I had been lucky because the tail section, where I had been, had spiralled down and had caught on some trees which had slowed its descent.

The villagers helped me across to the Mairie (the town hall) and laid me on the table. They sent for a doctor who came and looked at my leg but he said there was nothing he could do. I needed hospital treatment so they would have to tell the Germans that I was there so that I could have proper treatment. Meanwhile, he bandaged my leg up tightly and that eased the pain a bit.

Five Germans turned up to collect me and they knocked me about a bit, slapped me round the head mostly. One of the villagers protested so they hit him as well. I was manhandled into a truck and taken to hospital in Troyes where my leg and hip were seen to and I was cared for by the Sisters of Mercy. They really cared for me but I wasn't there long. I was collected by two German soldiers, bundled into the back seat of a car and taken to the Military Hospital in Paris. The treatment was different there but my leg had a chance to heal.

As soon as I could stand up, I was collected and taken for interrogation but I couldn't tell them what they wanted to know even if I had wanted to. I was then taken in a truck to Frankfurt, to the Airforce Interrogation unit there. It was questions all the time and again when they sent me on to another camp. They wanted to know why there was a third aerial on our plane. Our Lancaster had broken up in three distinct sections and it was the third aerial we carried that concerned my questioners. They gave me up as a bad job and I was sent to a P.O.W. (Prisoner of War) camp in Poland. Then we were moved again. It was a bit rough but we were better off than the Russians. We did receive red cross parcels from time to time that was more than the Russians did. Russia was not a member of the Geneva Conference so they were not entitled to them. We were released by the British army and were we pleased to see them.

Jack Worsford - Rear gunner.

• • • • • • •

Jack and Kitty Worsford

My uncle's name, Richard Johnson is on the local Roll of honour in Binbrook Church. That was where he was stationed during the war. He was attached to the Royal Australian Air Force, 460 Squadron. There were two other British crew members, Sergeant Fry and Sergeant Turnbull. Sergeant Riddell was a Canadian. David Barr was an Australian and so was Sergeant Hobbs. David Lloyd was the pilot and he was Australian too.

Richard was my mother's brother and she would never talk about him very much because it upset her to think about him. He had volunteered for the R.A.F. and volunteered for flying duties later on as a rear gunner. He loved the life and the crew was like a second family to him, my mother's as well because when he came home on leave he used to bring most of the crew with him. Well they were too far away from their own homes to go there so they came to ours. My mother would talk about the times when they were all in the house because it was fun from the minute they arrived. My mother's parents kept in touch with the crew's families. We're still in touch today. It's a friendship that has lasted a life time. The Australian and Canadian families used to send food parcels and my grand parents would have extra food to feed them. We had rationing here.

The family always called my uncle Dick but the crew never called him anything except Ginger.

Then it was May 3rd. 1944. Sergeant Riddell did not fly that day because he wasn't well. Another British airman, Sergeant Brian Wooten-Woolley, took his place.

Two days later, my grandparents received a telegram saying that Dick was missing. They learned that he had been killed two years later.

Diane Holywell. Niece of Flight Sergeant Richard Johnson

• • • • • • •

Sergeant Ackroyd parachuted to safety when his Lancaster was shot down, and joined the Resistance. He was captured by the Germans and handed over to the Gestapo who refused to treat him as a prisoner of war because he was wearing civilian clothes. His treatment in the hands of the Gestapo was so atrocious that he was asked to give evidence at the Nuremburg War trials.

My parents ran the newspaper shop in Barnetby and we delivered papers to Kirmington and Elsham Wolds and we were introduced to a lot of the airmen and women on the camps. I got to know a lot of them and it was a bit of luck when Frank was posted to Elsham Wolds.

Frank Holmes was my brother and he joined up along with my other brother just before war broke out. He didn't want to be ground crew. He wanted a bit of excitement and he volunteered to be a rear gunner.

Frank

He was a big chap was Frank, over six feet tall and he didn't find it too comfortable in the rear gunner's turret but he was fond of guns and he was good at using them. Shooting was part of his life before the war. He liked to do a bit of poaching out on Lord Yarborough's estate. Well you did in those days, didn't you?

I met all his crew. Geoff Madden was the pilot, the skipper. Don Charlwood was the navigator and the two other gunners.

I've kept in touch with them over the years but they're all over eighty now. Don Charlwood's had a stroke and some of the others aren't too well. They never talked about their raids that they'd been on. They had plenty of other things to talk about and life to them was to be lived. They were all for a bit of fun and having a laugh but there was this serious, caring side to them us well.

There was one day that they'd come

Frank's grave

back from a raid and Frank was tired but he got his gun and went off to get a bit of something for his dinner. He was after a pheasant. Well I suppose he wasn't as vigilant as he could have been but he got caught by the game keepers and they took his gun from him.

Frank was lost without his gun. It really upset him. I think most of the camp knew what had happened. His crew certainly did. They knew his habits and Don Charlwood always called him Poacher instead of Frank. My brother was really lost without his gun.

In the end the C.O. sent for him and asked him what had happened. He wrote to Lord Yarborough and explained that one of his men had returned from a particularly arduous raid and had gone out shooting on his land. He hadn't meant to do any harm but was in need of exercise and had gone out to do some shooting and the C.O. would appreciate it if his Lordship could see his way to returning the gun.

Lord Yarborough wrote back and said that he hadn't been aware of the situation and of course the gun would be returned and Sergeant Holmes must feel free to shoot over his land whenever he wished.

The gamekeepers had to give Frank his gun back and made a formal apology to him. Frank was cock a hoop to have the gun but the two gamekeepers were really down in the mouth at having to return it. They'd been after Frank for years. They used to come in the shop for their papers too and they told us that they would have really resented it if they hadn't liked Frank so much. He was that sort of man. He could get on with anyone. The funny thing about that incident was that Frank wasn't so keen to go out on his Lordship's estate now that he had permission to go.

The boys didn't talk about the raids but we could tell when things hadn't gone well. They'd be very quiet. My father would say they were tired but it was more than that. You could tell when they had had a bad experience. The raid on Mailly le Camp was one of those raids but we never knew they had been on that raid until years after the war. They went through a bad patch. There had been ten crews that had come down from County Durham and I knew them all. After a period of ten days, there were only three crews left, seven crews gone. That was forty nine men and I knew them all. Fortunately Frank's crew was one of the three.

They finished their tour soon after that and they were posted. The two Aussies went back to Australia. Frank was sent for training but it was too tame for him. He wanted the action so he went to join the pathfinders at Finningeley but he was only there a matter of days when he was sent down to Ely in Cambridgeshire and he was back as a rear gunner. On this particular raid, he changed places with the mid upper gunner because he was finding the rear gun turret was beginning to give him cramp. It was on that raid that they were shot down. They were bombing the railway sidings at Eccoville when they were shot down. There was only one survivor, the rear gunner, Flying Officer Armstrong.

We've been out to visit Frank's grave. It took us a long time to find out where he had been buried. It was forty years later but we still remembered him as he was. There was a service in the village Church and we weren't the only family members attending it. The surviving rear gunner was there and he stood up to say something during the service and before he could start speaking, the father of one of the crew members started sobbing. Even when someone helped him out of the Church, we could still hear him sobbing. Then I suppose grief is like that, real grief. It's always there. You never really forget. And he was right, he did lose his boy. They were all boys. Frank was 23 when he was killed and he was one of the oldest in the crew.

Mary Cawkwell - Sister of Flight Sergeant Frank Holmes

• • • • • • •

It was a dreadful night. We were woken by the noise of the Merlin engines and we took shelter where we could. Then bombs dropped on the camp and those of us who lived near could see men running towards the woods. Then the bombing stopped but we could still hear the sound of the engines although it was dulled by the bells and shouts in the camp. We knew something had been hit because we could see the flames and smell the smoke. Then we saw an aircraft exploding in the sky and hundreds of burning pieces scattered and fell. Then the Lancasters came again and they kept on coming. We could see them silhouetted against the sky and there were fighters amongst them. I thought they were Spitfires at first but they were German Junkers and Messerschmitts and they were shooting down the bombers. I saw three falling towards the ground before my mother shouted for me to get indoors. The first bombs had started to fall and the house shook. It was like an earthquake.

M.M. Mailly le Camp

• • • • • • •

218 German soldiers were killed, mostly N.C.O.s and were taken to Troyes for burial. 156 were injured. Prisoners of War and Frenchmen on forced labour were on the camp at the time and there were casualties amongst them but no figures were ever released. A number of soldiers had thought that the raid was over after the first bombs had fallen and had returned to the camp. They dived for shelter when the major part of the raid started. 80% of the barrack blocks, workshops and offices were destroyed and the other 20% damaged. 102 vehicles were lost including 37 tanks, The water tower was bombed releasing a flood of water which filled some trenches and drowned some of the men who were sheltering there. The German trenches were two metres deep and men found it difficult to get out of them in those conditions. From then on, lack of water made fighting the fires difficult. Fire engines were sent from local towns. The fuel dump blew up causing a fierce fire which engulfed a group of soldiers.

No bombs fell on the village.

Churchill had said that all French lives were to be spared but 14 people were killed when falling aircraft fell on them and a number of houses were damaged.

• • • • • • •

I volunteered for the fire service when I joined up. My second posting was to Elsham Wolds and I was there when they returned from the Mailly raid. Most of them had been shot up. It was a funny feeling standing there in the early morning and hear one of the Lancasters returning to base and know from the noise the engines were making that it had been damaged. We would stand there silently urging it to reach the runway and land safely. It was like that in the early hours of May 4th. 1944.

A fire tender always had to be present on the airfield. Our job was to save as many lives as possible but we were sometimes beaten back by the heat and the flames. One member of each crew wore a full asbestos suit and had been trained to try and rescue the trapped airmen. You could only wear the suit for ten minutes, fifteen at the most because the only available air was inside the suit. We would get as near as possible to the plane before we put on the hood. The crew would keep spraying water on us the whole time but it was often a desperate attempt in desperate circumstances.

We wore leather jerkins over our uniforms especially when attending a crash and the fires were so intense that bullets were firing from the gun turrets. One of the greatest dangers was when a plane crashed with a bomb on board. The flames and heat could set it off at any time. I thought the threat from the oxygen bottles was worse. There would be a nest of these near the cockpit and I would have to stand on them to try and rescue an airman while another fireman cooled them down with a spray of water. I knew they could blow up at any time and me with them but, once I was in that situation, my only thought was to reach the lads and get them out.

There were two Squadrons at Elsham Wolds and we had watched them leave for Mailly, a Lancaster lifting into the air every thirty seconds. We were still there when they returned and that was a tense time. You didn't let yourself think about those that hadn't returned but tried to do what you could to help the others and a lot of them were damaged. There was one plane with a Canadian crew that we had to chase down the runway because its brakes had failed completely. They pulled up O.K. but the crew must have set a record with the speed that they got out.

One plane crashed as it landed and the crew were killed except for the rear gunner. His turret had broken off completely. It landed some way away from the plane. The rear gunner had a broken leg.

Looking back on those days, I don't remember the bad times. I think of the companionship and working together for the same things and beliefs.

Typical light battle damage

Full asbestos rescue suit

If you didn't live in those times, I suppose it's difficult to understand the purpose, the determination and the hopes for the future that we all shared.

Reg Seward.

· · · · · · ·

A parachutist had come down near the village of Courboin and the military police arrived and started to question the children telling them that they would give them sweets if they would tell them where the English airman was hidden. Then they asked them if there had been strangers in the village but none of the children said anything. One of the boys had helped his father hide the Englishman but repeated that he hadn't seen anyone when the police carried on questioning. Nobody helped them and the Englishman stayed free until the allies reached our village.

· · · · · · ·

Sgt Geoff Gilbert

I was born at Burythorpe, a village near Malton in North Yorkshire. I was a rear gunner. I'd never wanted to be anything else except a rear gunner. My father worked for the hunt. He moved about a lot in his job and I was educated in Northumberland and Gloucestershire before we moved to Cambridgeshire in 1936. When I left school, I went to work with my father looking after the foxhounds. That was the custom of the day, following the same line of work as your father. When war broke out, I worked at a large Army Food Supply Unit near my home. I grew up knowing how to ride a horse and how to shoot. Shooting was my strength and I fancied manning those four guns in a rear turret. So I appled to join the RAF.

83

I completed my training on Ansoms We crewed up at the Operational Training Unit at Silverstone. We all collected in a hangar and the pilots selected their crews and Don Street approached me and asked me to join his. I had noticed Don. He looked reliable. He was older than most of the men in the hangar. He was 24. I've had a lucky life and I was lucky then. Don was a regular. He'd been a corporal fitter with 61 squadron and finished up as Flying Officer, D.F.C. in the same squadron. Some men are good at flying aeroplanes and some are good at operations. Don was one of the latter. He had soon assembled his crew and we developed an understanding and camaraderie that was to stand us in good stead. Some say that the crew became your family and I suppose in a way they did but the feeling was deeper than that. We worked as a group in conditions and experiences that were unique to the times.

Don was the pilot. The navigator was Dave Grant. He was Canadian. Douglas Boothby was the wireless operator and Charles Waghorn was the flight engineer. He was quiet and unflappable. Waggy had been a sergeant fitter in 1939. He was reliable and worked well with the crew but he kept himself to himself when we were on the ground. He was always smart, dressed like a new pin. We reckoned he had his eye on the C.O.'s daughter. Then there was Jock Haddon, a Scot. He was a scruffy little devil but he finished his career in the R.A.F. as a warrant officer and he was the smartest man in the camp by then.

I was on my own as a rear gunner. It was lonely and it could be cold but you didn't think of that. My job was to watch out for attacking fighters and shoot them down and I didn't rest for a minute. I was looking out all the time right until we were safely back at Skellingthorpe. You never knew when fighters would appear and you had to be ready for them. They had a habit of coming up to you from below especially if there was a light sky. Then the Lancaster would make an easy target because it was silhouetted in their sights. German fighters had upward pointing guns and we had to watch out for them. I didn't lose my concentration for a second., not even to reach for a flask of coffee. I tried not to look at the explosions on the ground in case the bright lights affected my eyesight and made it difficult for me to identify approaching German fighters. Sometimes a German fighter would follow us back to base. If the call, "Scatter bandits," was heard, we scattered. There were cases of returning aircraft being shot down when they were almost home and dry by one of these bandits.

50 Squadron was also stationed at Skellingthorpe and there was a lot of friendly rivalry between the two squadrons but there was no malice. We were young and high spirited and we did a lot of silly things like taking the station bell and leaving it in unusual places and borrowing underclothes from the W.A.A.F.s clothes line and hoisting them up the flag pole.

When the corporal came round to announce that there was a war on, we knew there was to be a raid that night and we invariably asked what were the cookies and cannes. Cookies were the 4,000 pound bombs we would be carrying and cannes were the incendiaries that would be included in the bomb loads. We would also want to know how much fuel had been put in the tanks. That would give us some idea of where we would be flying. 2,000 gallons and 1,000lb cookies invariably meant a raid on Germany, 1,500 gallons was mostly France. Maximum fuel and fewer bombs meant a long trip. The corporal would continue – "meal 18.00 hours, briefing 19.00 hours, take off 22.00 hours."

We would all attend the main briefing. Our target was pointed out and red tape would mark our routes to and from it. Then we would divide into smaller groups for our own individual briefings. I joined the gunner leader.

Then we would draw our kit and parachute packs. These were handed out by W.A.A.F.s. The first time I collected mine, I noticed a mug of water on the side and I asked for a drink. I took three sips of the water and put the mug down and I did that every time I went to collect my parachute, took just three sips of water. It became a ritual. The girls would have the mug of water waiting on the table for me. A lot of the men had lucky charms or performed some actions which they thought would bring them safely home again. Some crews piddled on the wheels of their aircraft but we didn't do that. The crews hated change. They would be uneasy if one of their crew was ill and they had to have a substitute in his place. They would see that as bad luck. To a certain extent, some of the men blamed the pathfinders for the problems at the raid on Mailly. We were using a different kind of marking for the target and some of the men didn't like it. 617 were low level markers. It was different to the method that had been used before and some of the crews were hesitant, almost superstitious about the change. I had a fox mascot. Mother had bought me it to remind me of *home. I used to take the fox with me and put the name of our target on him. When we had completed our last tour, one of the other rear gunners asked me if he could take the fox with him and I gave it to him. He didn't come back. You can't swop your luck.*

We would be driven out to our planes in buses. The drivers were W.A.A.F.s. We couldn't have existed without them. The W.A.A.F.s worked really hard and they virtually ran the station. Each crew would be dropped near their Lancaster, ours was Y for Yoke, and we would stand around waiting while the skipper completed all the checks. It would be standing on the apron ready for us, fuelled and bombed up. The ground organisation was excellent and we got to know our ground crew. Everything would have been checked, the engines, air-frame, controls, radio and radar units, compasses, bombing gear, electrics and armaments. Guns were cleaned and minor defects rectified before the night's loads were hoisted into the racks and the fuel pumped in.

We would get into the plane, find our places and prepare for the flight.

The engines would start up. There is nothing like the sound of the Merlin engines and the throb of a Lancaster. Then we would be moving in a long line of bombers towards the end of the runway, ready for a signal from the runway caravan for take off. I would close my eyes and say a little prayer as we rose higher into the air, "Please God, don't let me be burned or branded." I'm not a religious man but that prayer was important to me at that time.

We flew our whole tour together. We were on one raid to Gelsenkirchen near Essen when we were coned (caught in the searchlights) for eleven minutes and we couldn't get away from them. The blue white master beam had latched on to us and, almost immediately, four or five white searchlight beams were following our flight as well. Inside the plane, everything was a blinding glare. "Shoot down the beam," the skipper had ordered but that was easier said than done. Thankfully there weren't any German fighters in the air at that moment but there was plenty of flak and Don was twisting and turning to get out of the light. The experienced pilots kept well away when they saw another aircraft caught by a searchlight. We did. We knew how easy it was for the beam to transfer to another plane in the vicinity. We were caught in the beam for eleven minutes and eleven minutes was a long time when you're airborne.

"Hang on, everybody," Don said, "we're going down," and he

rammed the control column forward and dropped the port wing in a diving turn to the left.

The altimeter unwound losing height by 500feet-1000 – 1500 – 2000. He rolled the aircraft over to a starboard turn still losing height, 2500 – 3000 – 3500 – 3700 feet and then they were gone as suddenly as they came and there was blackness all round. The pilot reached forward, turned on the orange shaded cockpit light and hauled the aircraft up and back on course.

It took a while for my eyes to become accustomed to the change from penetrating light to dark.

Another time we were bombing Brest. There were lots of searchlights and explosions. We had just left the target when the Lanc went into a steep dive and I found myself looking at the sky. We were going straight down and I thought we had been hit and it was the end of the road. Strangely, I felt detached from it all. I didn't feel frightened. It was almost as if it was happening to another person. Then suddenly we had straightened out. I'd been thrown about a bit and I sorted myself out and said, "What was that for Streetie?"

"I thought we'd better get out of there quick," he replied.

"God," Dave Argent's Canadian accent commented, "I never knew there were so many nuts and bolts in a Church roof."

We had plenty of flak holes but the ground crew patched them up with biscuit tins. We were badly shot up over Stuttgart and one of our engines was shot out. We limped home and were a long way behind the rest of the flight. We didn't expect the corporal in the mess to have waited up for us with our cups of cocoa and bread and cheese. She was a right tartar. Nobody tried to argue with her. But she was waiting for us.

"I knew you'd get back," she said as we went in. She got on with our crew. We could generally get round her. Sometimes when there was no raid and we'd gone into Nottingham, we often wouldn't get back until four in the morning and we'd be hungry and make for the mess. "Couldn't those birds you've been with give you a bite to eat," she would say but she generally found us something.

We had to be alert all the time we were airborne and the skipper never questioned us and reacted immediately. "Skipper, nightfighter coming in to starboard," and Don, would be diving out of its path in a second.

We were on one raid when there was a full moon and the moonlight *reflected against the haze. The light was at the brightest I could remember it and it was difficult to keep watching out for enemy fighters because the reflected light was so bright.*

"Skipper, I've picked up a bandit at 1200yards astern and to port." *The wireless operator was watching his small radar screen.*

"Thanks. Gunners, sharp look out."

The skipper's order wasn't necessary but it established the rapport.

"1,000 yards now, Skipper. The closing rate isn't high," *and a few minutes later,* "800yards."

"Any sign of it, rear gunner?"

"Can't see a thing."

"Mid upper?"

"Not yet, Skipper."

"600 yards, still there," *called the wireless operator*

"Gillie, Jock, any sign yet?" *the pilot was getting anxious.*

"500 yards, still there," *came the steady voice of the wireless operator,* "400 yards, no change. Could be one of ours with his IFF (Identification Friend or Foe) not switched on."

"Let's find out. I'm turning 90 degrees to starboard. Now."

Don realised he was crossing the bomber stream as he swung on to the new heading so he held the plane at a steady altitude to lessen the chance of a collision. He needed to identify the aircraft that was shadowing us. The poor visibility left no time for doubt. The gunners would shoot or be shot at the first glimpse. We were ready. We stayed on the new heading for several minutes when the wireless operator's voice broke the tense silence, "I've still got him Skip, right behind, 400 yards."

"O.K. I'm turning left back on to course now. Any sign Gill, Jock?"

"300 yards, 250," *Doug's voice was full of anxiety.*

Then, "Got him, corkscrew port. Go, go go." *I had a clear view of him and, as the Lancaster dropped down in a turning dive, I added,* "it's a Junkers 88"

He hadn't fired at us. The evasive action had been too quick and he had lost us in the haze. When some 950 feet had unwound on the altimeter, the pilot turned the aircraft 60 degrees to starboard and into a climbing turn.

"Where is he, Doug?"

*"He's moving to rear, across to port side about 300 yards, 200…
.."*

The fighter was changing its position rapidly as the bomber
followed an evasive pattern.

"Have you got it gunners?"

"Corkscrew port," I started but Jock interrupted.

"Hold it Skipper, hold it."

The Lancaster was still climbing with a slight turn to starboard.
Now the pilot held it straight and level. Then it all happened in a split
second. The Browning guns rattled.

"He's breaking away to port," the wireless operator called.

"He's going down rapidly."

"He's on fire. We got him," shouted Jock.

"Are you sure?" queried the pilot.

"We've got him. He's on fire ," I shouted.

"He's hit the deck and there's two parachutes," the wireless
operator was standing up with his head in the astrodome and shouting
excitedly.

"Where is it?"

We were only too keen to tell him.

*"Good show. Well done. Log the time and the position Dave. One
Junkers 88 destroyed. Settle down now fellas and let's get home."*

Back at base on the dispersal pan with the parking drills completed
and the engines stopped, we felt quiet and drained. It was quietly
suggested to the ground crew that they could add a swastika to the
bomb symbols painted on the side of the fuselage. Then we made our
way to the debriefing room. We grabbed a mug of tea, perhaps with a
shot of rum before we sat down with the debriefing officer. The crew
were weary, war weary as were so many of the other crews.

It was some time after this that I heard I had been awarded
the D.F.M. (the Distinguished Flying Medal) and was to go to
Buckingham Palace to receive it. I think my mother was more excited
than me especially about going to Buckingham Palace. The three of
us, Mum Dad and me, went to Kings Cross by train. We had ordered a
taxi but it failed to turn up. We waited for a while then went for a bus.
I asked if it went to the Palace and the conductor told me that it did.
It took us to Crystal Palace. Well we got back to Central London and
we started to run down the Mall. We were late. A car pulled up and we
were told to jump in by a full General with his own personal driver. We
rolled up to Buckingham Palace in style.

Then it was May 3rd. 1944 and the corporal came round announcing that there was a war on and we knew there was a raid that night. By this time we were more than two thirds through our tour and we were beginning to feel confident that we would complete it. The target that night was Mailly le Camp and there was nothing in the briefing to blunt that confidence. It was a straightforward bombing raid and no problems were expected. Targets over France were proving so much easier than those over Germany that it had been announced in April that we needed to complete three raids over France before we could claim one towards our total of completed operations.

There was tension as we waited on the apron to climb in to Lancaster Y for Yoke. There always was before a raid and men eased that tension in different ways, some by making jokes, others by going to one side and having a quiet moment on their own. Somehow the tension was not so high that night. There wasn't expected to be any trouble. Some even referred to it as a milk run.

Both squadrons from Skellingthorpe were on the raid, 61 and 50. As it happened we were the last to lift off. Once we were in the air, we became more relaxed. We all had work to do and we needed to concentrate. I don't know if Don was suspicious that the raid was not going to be as easy as expected but he took evading action as we crossed the channel. "Enemy coast ahead," the navigator announced. There was no emotion in his voice. We weaved our way to the target. Our golden rule was that we could expect trouble whenever we were over enemy territory and we were to be ready for it. The approach to the target was trouble free. Then I heard the navigator's voice saying that there was no need for his services. He could see the target ahead. I couldn't see a thing at the tail end of the plane but they carried on their chatter for my benefit. I was taken aback to hear that a Lancaster had exploded in the air and that there were fighters amongst the bombers. It seemed that a number of Lancasters had not yet cleared the target area and we had to wait off while they went in and bombed. There's always a danger in circumstances like that that a bomber can drop its bombs on a friendly plane beneath it or that two Lancasters can collide. We had a near miss ourselves. The navigator was the pilot's eyes. He was reliable, observant and accurate.

"Look ahead, Skipper," he said and immediately the pilot lifted the Lancaster up. We missed the plane that had been flying in front of us by a matter of yards.

"I saw the rivets on that one, Skip," came the Canadian drawl.

Don asked the navigator for a course away from the chaos and we circled further out. When we returned to the target, the skies were not so congested but there was still plenty of activity and our crew was silenced as we saw another bomber being hit and diving towards the ground.

We were flying towards a lot of trouble. There was no mention of that as each of us in turn reported to the skipper. The navigator announced, "Coming to target," and the bomb aimer took over from him. The navigator gave him the most recent estimate of the prevailing wind and the bomb aimer would start to adjust the position at which the bombs were to be dropped. The wind can affect the direction at which the bomb travels as well as the aircraft. The run up to, through and out of the target area was a disciplined drill. We were some ten miles out from the final run in. I was searching the skies for enemy fighters as we approached and listened through my headphones as the bomb aimer's voice gave instruction to the pilot. Then the order came for us to go in and bomb.

"Bomb doors open. Left, left steady. Right to starboard. Bombs away. O.K. Skipper."

He didn't have to say that the bombs had been dropped. The aircraft was always much lighter to fly after the release of the bomb load. We had been carrying a, 4000 pound cookie and 16 x 500 pound G.P.s (General Purpose) bombs. We felt them go. We had to wait about thirty seconds for the target photo flash. Then the announcement came, "Bomb doors closed." We should have bombed at 00.04 hours. We went in at 00.34. We were 30 minutes late. We were the last aircraft to bomb. The four Merlin engines were harmonised. The pressures and temperatures were as they should be. Don's voice, with as much expression as I had ever heard him use on a raid, said, "Let's get the hell out of here."

Although we had been doing our own jobs, we were aware of the devastation going on around us. We could see burning aircraft on the ground, black smoke drifting like funeral pyres and, even as we turned, another Lancaster exploded to our starboard side and there were still the German fighters flying amongst us. As we turned for home, we picked up a Meschersmitt. Don dived immediately and we lost it. We didn't wait around. Don told the navigator to plot a new course. We didn't want to stay too close to the mainstream because some of the German fighters were trailing them. We were the last to bomb at Mailly and because I was rear gunner I was the last airman to leave.

The skipper asked the navigator how far to the coast and repeated the question every few minutes. We were all relieved as we reached the Channel and realised that we were on our own. We avoided the Channel

60 years on, Tom Bennett, Charles Wearmouth, ML Clement, President of the Mailly Associa-tion, Geoff Gilbert. Pat Furlong is standing behind M Clement.

Islands. They were deadly. They were so heavily defended, particularly at Sark. We landed at Skellingthorpe, went for the debriefing and went to bed. It wasn't until the next morning that we found how many planes and men had been lost. Our Squadron was lucky. They all returned but 50 Squadron lost four of their Lancasters. 42 aircraft lost and their crews with them.

When we finished our tour, we were posted. The crew had lived and worked together and now we were being sent to different parts of the universe. We shook hands and said goodbye and went to our new posting. That was what war was like especially in the R.A.F. We were constantly moving on. I didn't meet some of my crew or hear what had happened to them until thirty years later.

I was still in Bomber Command but I was attached to the navy and sent to Plymouth

Sergeant Geoff Gilbert – Rear gunner

Children from the Holt School Skellingthorpe maintain a close relationship with 50 Squadron

· · · · · · ·

Post operative briefings and reports show how confused things had been.

106 Squadron reported, "No W/T messages received before bombing. R/T messages were contradictory"

44 Squadron, " No instructions received on R/T or W/T. Aircraft bombed because they saw other aircraft going in to bomb."

630 Squadron, "Marking precise and accurate. R/T bad."

49 Squadron, 9 Squadron, 50 Squadron and 207 Squadron all commended the accuracy of the red spot fires and Squadron Leader Blore-Jones of 207 Squadron added this rider, "Yellow T.I. on datum. No orders from Controller. Complete chaos in target area. Controller inefficient and crew discipline bad."

There was a further comment from 49 Squadron, "Congestion over target to a degree of suicide. 18 – 25 minutes wait for order to bomb."

· · · · · · ·

93

COPY OF THE OFFICIAL REPORT FROM
H.Q. STAFF 5 GROUP, ST VINCENTS, GRANTHAM.
MAY 7.1944 STATES:

"The marking was prompt and accurate but RT communication was badly interrupted by an RT station broadcasting American news and the WT transmitter in the leader's aircraft was at least 30 k.c.s off frequency.

Although practically the whole of the target has been severely damaged, the main weight of the attack has fallen on the large compact group of MT and barrack buildings. Out of 47 NH buildings at the north side of the site, not one has escaped damage, 34 being totally destroyed. A larger group of 144 barrack buildings have also suffered very severely, 47 being destroyed and many of the remainder damaged.

The workshops to the south of this group are more dispersed and lie outside the greatest concentration of craters. Many have, nevertheless, been destroyed and scarcely any have escaped damage. A second group of MT buildings to the east has suffered similarly. Further to the east of the built area, the ammunition dump and the range have both been hit."

• • • • • • •

There were six night fighter stations within 100 miles of the route that the bombers were taking. Three German aces were at these stations and were quickly in the air to attack the Lancasters. Helmet Bergman claimed five kills as did Martin Drewes who was stationed at Leon. Dietrich Schmidt was also stationed at Leon and he claimed three kills. They flew NJGs, (Nachtjagdgeschwaders). Their night fighters were equipped with airborne radar to detect their quarry and some were equipped with upward pointing guns called schragge musik (jazz music) which allowed them to fire into the Lancaster's blind spot beneath the plane. Fighters from as far away as Holland and Northern Germany were alerted but were not needed.

Those who flew on these missions knew that they were risking their lives. It was their job. This was not the case of the brave French people who helped the airmen who landed in their country to evade the Germans. They knew that if they were caught, they would face deportation or even death, yet they didn't think of that as they sheltered the men. It was the same for those who fought with the Resistance. They were very brave people. We wish to remember the following people in particular and apologize for the many others that we have not included, some who said they did such a little. In such circumstances, a little could be a lot.

Mme Roillard secretary of the Mailly le Camp Association is taught how to play by RAF Bugler, Paul Sutton.

Monsieur and Madame DuPont
Mesdamoiselles Chambullons.
Monsieur and Madame Derivery
Monsieur P. Ferat
Doctor Bouvier
Madame DuQuesne.
Monsieur and Madame Patris.
Monsieur Jenson
Monsieur and Madame Advet
Madame Deguilly
Monsieur R. Meunier
Monsieur Dupuy
Monsieur Morand
Monsieur Piquet
Monsieur Jacob
Monsieur J. Renant
Dr Merat
Madame Cartignol
Monsieur and Madame Tisserand
Monsieur Doyselet
Monsieur Gillot
Monsieur and Madame Collet
Monsieur and Madame Dore
Monsieur and Madame Dormont
Madame Bertin
Madame Preano
Monsieur Boyon
Monsieur Demey and, of course, Praz and his team and all the others who worked with the Resistance.

EPILOGUE

Flight Sergeant Nigel Lacey-Johnson a navigator of 101 Squadron (LM467) was one of the airmen killed in the early hours of May 4th., 1944. in the skies above Mailly le Camp. His parents received a telegram telling them that their son was missing from bomber operations over Europe. Some ten years later, Nigel's wife and son visited his grave. Then, like so many families who had lost loved ones during the Second World War, his family accepted that he had been shot down and killed on this particular raid. It was not until his brother, Lt. Col. Lionel Lacey-Johnson visited Voue, where his brother was buried, that people started to look at this particular raid and to ask questions about it. He himself had been seventeen years of age when the raid took place. Now he was able to gain a vivid picture of what happened

Lionel questioned people who had been alive at the time of the raid and had spoken to one of the men who had collected the bodies and taken them to the Church yard for burial. Their graves had been marked with simple wooden crosses until the Commonwealth War Graves Commission took them over in 1949. Four headstones mark their resting place along with the body of Flight Sergeant Bodsworth of 166 Squadron who was also killed that night.

When he returned to England, Lt. Col. Lionel Lacey-Johnson wrote to the Mayor of Voue, Monsieur Louis Clement. It seemed that the Mayor was keen to have a reception for the relatives of those who had been killed that night, so Lionel contacted as many people as was possible and, with the assistance and help of the French army, the reception took place in May, 1987, the 43rd anniversary of the raid..

Following this, mayors of several other villages where airmen had been been buried wanted to have a similar reception. Monsieur Clement's dearest wish was that there should be a permanent memorial to these men. Thus the Mailly Association was started and I think all of us who have attended a ceremony at Mailly le Camp will realise what a special occasion this has become and how a simple visit by Lt. Col. Lacey-Johnson enquiring about his brother has developed into something that is unique. We have come to appreciate the care and consideration of Monsieur Clement as Chairman of the Society and Madame Huguette Rouillard, the Secretary as well as the members of the committee and the co-operation of the French Army Authority at the training camp. It was from these beginnings that the annual ceremony evolved. 101 Squadron has always supported this occasion, parading the standard and colours and a bugler to play the Last Post.

It is not only the airmen we remember on that day but we also think of the French people who had faced the German occupation for four years and were prepared to risk their own lives to help some of our airmen. In the summer of 1944, the Germans perpetrated some horrific acts as they retreated and these are marked by a number of plaques throughout the region.

In May, 1991, Group Captain Leonard Cheshire, V.C. unveiled the memorial to those who died at the raid on Mailly le Camp in 1944. It was well attended by veterans and their families, members of the French Resistance as well as many interested and local people. Leonard Cheshire gave his address in both English and French. He also attended the ceremony in 1992.

From that date the interest in the raid has increased, thanks to the Mailly Committee and the hospitality of the French army. Inevitably the number of veterans attending has decreased over the years but the public interest has not waned. It is good to know that the memory of those that took part in this raid is still being remembered, not only by the descendants of those who flew that day but others who have an interest in Bomber Command.

The men who flew in this raid look on the raid at Mailly le Camp as the start of D Day because this was when Operation Pointblank was extended to attack targets that could hinder the soldiers' advance once they had landed on the beaches. The Panzer Division at Mailly was one of those threats.

This increase of interest is shared in England.

When Mrs Shirley Westrop, who had been the secretary of the Elsham Wolds Society decided that it was time to retire, members of the local community decided that they did not want to lose the memories and history of those times. It is now a strong society that welcomes anyone who shares their interest. The airfield is now owned by the Anglian Water Company who has set a room aside for a museum. Regular meetings are held in the local village of Barnetby.

Metheringham Airfield has reverted to farmland and local farmers, Peter and Zena Scoley have preserved some of the R.A.F. buildings one of which houses a small museum. The Friends of Metheringham Airfield is an active Society which is a member of The British Aviation Preservation Council.

East Kirkby has become The Lincolnshire Aviation Heritage Centre, a well known museum where pride of place is given to the Lancaster "Just Jane". The centre was started by the Panton brothers, Fred and Harold, in memory of their brother, Christopher, who was shot down over Europe on the Nuremburg raid. There is a family atmosphere here and anyone who has an interest in those times can be sure of a warm welcome, but be sure you have a couple of hours or more to spare.

All the airfields in Lincolnshire from which aircraft flew on May 3rd 1944 have a plaque to mark their history. It is great to know that the memories are shared by both countries on either side of the Channel.

TO LIVE ON IN THE HEARTS OF THOSE WE LOVE IS NOT TO DIE.

*The memorial at
Mailly le Camp*

POSTSCRIPT

Leonard Cheshire was one of the special kind of men that war produces. He was quiet and thoughtful, a perfectionist that would not tolerate second best. Within ten minutes of meeting him, you knew that here was a man you could trust.

He was already thinking of his life after the war and the raid on Mailly le Camp was one of those that strengthened his resolve and determination to open the now famous Cheshire Homes to help those who had suffered and were less fortunate than himself.

It was while he was visiting Cheshire Homes in Australia that he was accosted on three occasions by men who blamed him for the casualties at Mailly. They wouldn't listen to him and he was very distressed by these meetings. He contacted me when he returned to England and I conducted a lot of personal research on his behalf, both in the archives in the Public Record Office at Kew and with the two surviving Mosquito pilots. (Pat Kelly had been killed on a later Dortmund- Ems Canal operation with 49 Squadron while filling the post of Staff Navigation Officer at East Kirkby)

I would like this opportunity to make our position clear. None of us (617 target marking crews) were aware of any VHF interference by any outside broadcasting source. Our orders were to accurately mark the target and return to base and this is what we did. We had been asked to do this because we had more experience than 627 Squadron in marking confined targets. At the time we were operating with our own Squadron on Operation Taxable (the D day spoof) and we were taken off it for this one raid.

The first wave controller was Wing Commander Deane of 83 Squadron. He was adamant that it was VHF interference that was present which prevented him from communicating with the aircraft to start bombing. He had instructed the Wireless Operator to give the "Start bombing" message but it failed to get though

Another contributing factor was the laying of the yellow datum point and the instruction to circle this point if there was any delay. All the crews were fully trained. They could be expected to keep station in a waiting area without these sort of aids. It was an open invitation to the German night fighters.

Squadron Leader Breakspear from Binbrook was the Master Bomber for No. I group the second wave. He was delayed by No 5 Group failing to clear the target area.

When Cheshire saw how the raid was developing, he tried to abort it, but failed. I hope this sets the records straight.

Sqld Tom Bennett. Navigator 617 Sqdn

Geoffrey Leonard Cheshire

RAFA Colour bearer and party at Mailly le Camp

Molly Burkett with Air Vice Marshal, the Venerable Brian Lucas, M L Clement Chairman of the Mailly Le Camp Association and Mme Rouillard (Secretary)

A Tribute to those who failed to return (Below)

The cemetary at Oeuilly

Inevitably, we lost many of the friends that we made among the crews and, deep down, this caused some feeling of remorse especially when we were assisting in a Court of Adjustment. This was a job we all hated. We felt we were intruding into other peoples' lives who were not there to protect themselves. A Court of Adjustment was the name given to the disposal of the personal possessions of aircrew who were missing or killed. It involved collecting all their belongings and sorting out service equipment and returning items of a personal nature to their families. We had to rifle through lockers, drawers, wallets, even pockets. Sometimes a letter would have been left to send on to a loved one. There was no joking when we did this. It was an unhappy, intrusive task and we hated it.

P.O. Beechey.

F/S N Reilly RAFVER (third from left) - KIA

S/L H Swanston RAFVR and crew - 103 Squadron - KIA 4th May 1944

ROLL OF HONOUR

Ainsworth S.W.
Andrews R.W.
Applegarth K.
Archard T.E.
Arnold R.F.
Atkinson C.
Bailey E.
Bailey J.
Baker G.
Barber G.C.
Barker F.W.
Barker R.
Barkway P.J.W.
Barr D.R.
Barr S.J.
Baskerville N.G.
Batt W.
Bearne H.W.V.
Bell C.

Bell F.J.
Bengston J.
Berry J.
Bishop N.R.
Bisset D.
Black H.P.
Blair G.A.
Blake E.G.
Bodsworth A.W.
Boreham C.J.
Borton E.E
Bowles A.J.
Boyd R.H.
Bradburn J.L.
Brady H.G. DFM
Bremner J.M.
Brooks A.G.
Brown C.T.
Burgess F.
Burgess J.R.
Burton A.W.
Burton F.W.
Carlton A.E. DFC
Carlyle DFM
Carter J.D.
Casey G.F.
Chandler J.
Charlton E.H.
Clayton T.R.
Close D.E.
Cockburn J.T.
Coldicott D.J.
Coote G.A.
Cottrell E.C.
Crawford R.J.
Cro D.H.
Croft C.W.
Crook R.D.
Crooks H.M.

Cross R.J.
Dance R.K.
Dand R.M.
Dane E.J.
Dickson C.
Dixon W.D.
Drew T.J.
Dudley C.G.
Duffy M.H.
Dye K.R.
Earl J.C. DFM
Elgar W.R.
Ellis J.
Ellis R.
Ellsmere R.O.
Escritt B.
Evans G. W.
Fisher N.J.
Footman W.A.C.
Forden H.H.
Fraser D.C.
Fry H.J.G.
Fry P.D.
Fryer G.
Furniss O.S.
Garner K.
Garrod R.S.
Gay C.S.
Gilpen G.E.
Glover F.
Godfrey R.F.
Gorman J.J.
Gracey R.J.
Graham C.G.
Grain A.J. DFM
Green R.A.
Gritty M.J.
Hackett M.J.
Hadden D.A.

Haddock R.E.
Handley A.
Hanson R.S.
Harris W.A.
Hatton N.
Hayhurst T.S.
Healy J.
Higgins P.
Hobbs R.H.
Hobson G.H.
Hodson A.A.H.
Hogan R.E.
Hogg G.
Holden J.E.
Holloway J.H.
Hooper J.W.
Hopkins M.
Houlden E.
Housden E.G.
Hoxford F.C.
Hughes L.F.
Hull W.E. DFC
Hutchinson E.S.
Ineson J.F.
Jackson D.S. DFC
Johnson J.G.
Johnson L.
Johnson M.A.
Johnson P.I.
Johnson R.A.
Jones D.G.
Jones E.C.
Jones H.C.
Jones W.T.
Joy F.H. DFM
Keard J.A.
Kenny J.F.
Lacey-Johnson N.A.
Larman K.T.

Liebscher J.M.B.
Lissett L.H.
Lloyd N.D.L.
Long G.
MacFarlane R.E.
Mac Kenzie H.F.
Maltby J.H. DFM
Margetts L.C.
Martin D.C. MD
Martin R,H.
Martin W.B.
Maxwell W.C.
McA McGaw N.
McCallum A.A.
McCool J.
McD Davies
McNaught D.H.
Medway L.F.
Metcalfe E.A.
Milton K.B.
Molzan O.
Moore A.B.
Moore J.E.
Moran J.
Morey J.K.
Moriarty D.
Muir K.W.A.
Myers W.M.E.
Naismith F.F.
Naylor A.
Newton A.J. DFM
Nolan A.W.
Norton G.H.
O'Neill G.E.
Oldfield J.
Oliver M.R.
Ormrod J.H.
Oulton T.
Owen K.W.

Pappajohn A.P.

Parker N.F.

Payne S.W.

Pecket H.M.

Pickford H

Ranger J.W.

Rankin J.R.

Read K.N.

Reid J.J.

Reilly N.P.

Reynolds J.A.

Ridd H.G.

Riddle H.A.

Ridgway A.J.

Rodway S.J.

Rogers W.J.H.

Roper V.R.

Rowe S.J.

Russel R.

Russell S.R.

Sallis J.H.

Scrivener R.A.F.

Searle F.C.

Shannon A.M

Shaw J.W

Shenton A.C

Short C.D.A

Simpson A.P

Skellorn H.

Smart J. W.

Smith J. C.

Smith N. A.

Sneddon R. A.

Spowart J. R.

Staniland P. A.

Stanley J.

Stannett E. F.

Stephensen C. E.

Steward J. E.

Stone E. A.
Stuart I. F.
Sumner L.
Sutton J. A. J.
Swanston H.
Sykes T. W.
Tailby R. J.
Thompson W. H.
Turnbull J. G.
Vale L. R.
Wadsworth D. A. DFC
Waites J.
Walker W. R.
Walter F. G.
Walton C. R. F.
Ward J. B.
Ward R. J.
Warnock G. R.
Warren H.
Warren K. R.
Watts R. H.
Weaver P. J.
Webster R.
Weller R. D.
Whalley R.
Wheeler M. T.
Whipp S.
White J. W.
White T. C.
Whitelock C.
Widger W. H. DFM
Wilkins S. C.
Wilkinson J.
Willes S. H.
Williams H. E.
Williams J. A.
Wilson R. A.
Wilson R. D. DFM
Wilson S.
Winstanley T. S.
Woods J. G.
Wootton-Wooley B. T.